From Whose Bourne

Robert Barr

Contents

FROM WHOSE BOURNE

BY

Robert Barr

*TO
AN HONEST MAN
AND
A GOOD WOMAN*

CHAPTER I.

M y dear," said William Brenton to his wife, "do you think I shall be missed if I go upstairs for a while? I am not feeling at all well."

"Oh, I'm so sorry, Will," replied Alice, looking concerned; "I will tell them you are indisposed."

"No, don't do that," was the answer; "they are having a very good time, and I suppose the dancing will begin shortly; so I don't think they will miss me. If I feel better I will be down in an hour or two; if not, I shall go to bed. Now, dear, don't worry; but have a good time with the rest of them."

William Brenton went quietly upstairs to his room, and sat down in the darkness in a rocking chair. Remaining there a few minutes, and not feeling any better, he slowly undressed and went to bed. Faint echoes reached him of laughter and song; finally, music began, and he felt, rather than heard, the pulsation of dancing feet. Once, when the music had ceased for a time, Alice tiptoed into the room, and said in a quiet voice--

"How are you feeling, Will? any better?"

"A little," he answered drowsily. "Don't worry about me; I shall drop off to sleep presently, and shall be all right in the morning. Good night."

He still heard in a dreamy sort of way the music, the dancing, the laughter; and gradually there came oblivion, which finally merged into a dream, the most strange and vivid vision he had ever experienced. It seemed to him that he sat again in the rocking chair near the bed. Although he knew the room was dark, he had no difficulty in seeing everything perfectly. He heard, now quite plainly, the music and dancing downstairs, but what gave a ghastly significance to his dream was the sight of his own person on the bed. The eyes were half open, and the face was drawn and rigid. The colour of the face was the white, greyish tint of death.

"This is a nightmare," said Brenton to himself; "I must try and wake myself." But he seemed powerless to do this, and he sat there looking at his own body while the night wore on. Once he rose and went to the side of the bed. He seemed to have reached it merely by wishing himself there, and he passed his hand over the face, but no feeling of touch was communicated to him. He hoped his wife would come and rouse him from this fearful semblance of a dream, and, wishing this, he found himself standing at her side, amidst the throng downstairs, who were now merrily saying good-bye. Brenton tried to speak to his wife, but although he was conscious of speaking, she did not seem to hear him, or know he was there.

The party had been one given on Christmas Eve, and as it was now two o'clock in the morning, the departing guests were wishing Mrs. Brenton a merry Christmas. Finally, the door closed on the last of the revellers, and Mrs. Brenton stood for a moment giving instructions to the sleepy servants; then, with a tired sigh, she turned and went upstairs, Brenton walking by her side until they came to the darkened room, which she entered on tiptoe.

"Now," said Brenton to himself, "she will arouse me from this appalling dream." It was not that there was anything dreadful in the dream itself, but the clearness with which he saw everything, and the fact that his mind was perfectly wide awake, gave him an uneasiness which he found impossible to shake off.

In the dim light from the hall his wife prepared to retire. The horrible thought struck Brenton that she imagined he was sleeping soundly, and was anxious not to awaken him--for of course she could have no realization of the nightmare he was in--so once again he tried to communicate with her. He spoke her name over and over again, but she proceeded quietly with her preparations for the night. At last she crept in at the other side of the bed, and in a few moments was asleep. Once more Brenton struggled to awake, but with no effect. He heard the clock strike three, and then four, and then five, but there was no apparent change in his dream. He feared that he might be in a trance, from which, perhaps, he would not awake until it was too late. Grey daylight began to brighten the window, and he noticed that snow was quietly falling outside, the flakes noiselessly beating against the window pane. Every one slept late that morning, but at last he heard the preparations for breakfast going on downstairs--the light clatter of china on the table, the rattle of the grate; and, as he thought of these things, he found himself in the dining-room, and saw the trim little maid, who still yawned every now and then, laying the plates in their places. He went upstairs again, and stood watching the sleeping face of his wife. Once she raised her hand above her head, and he thought she was going to awake; ultimately her eyes opened, and she gazed for a time at the ceiling, seemingly trying to recollect the events of the day before.

"Will," she said dreamily, "are you still asleep?"

There was no answer from the rigid figure at the front of the bed. After a few moments she placed her hand quietly over the sleeper's face. As she did so, her startled eyes showed that she had received a shock. Instantly she sat upright in bed, and looked for one brief second on the face of the sleeper beside her; then, with a shriek that pierced the stillness of the room, she sprang to the floor.

"Will! Will!" she cried, "speak to me! What is the matter with you? Oh, my God! my God!" she cried, staggering back from the bed. Then, with shriek after shriek, she ran blindly through the hall to the stairway, and there fell fainting on the floor.

CHAPTER II.

William Brenton knelt beside the fallen lady, and tried to soothe and comfort her, but it was evident that she was insensible.

"It is useless," said a voice by his side.

Brenton looked up suddenly, and saw standing beside him a stranger. Wondering for a moment how he got there, and thinking that after all it was a dream, he said--

"What is useless? She is not dead."

"No," answered the stranger, "but *you* are."

"I am what?" cried Brenton.

"You are what the material world calls dead, although in reality you have just begun to live."

"And who are you?" asked Brenton. "And how did you get in here?"

The other smiled.

"How did *you* get in here?" he said, repeating Brenton's words.

"I? Why, this is my own house."

"Was, you mean."

"I mean that it is. I am in my own house. This lady is my wife."

"Was," said the other.

"I do not understand you," cried Brenton, very much annoyed. "But, in any case, your presence and your remarks are out of place here."

"My dear sir," said the other, "I merely wish to aid you and to explain to you anything that you may desire to know about your new condition. You are now free from the incumbrance of your body. You have already had some experience of the additional powers which that riddance has given you. You have also, I am afraid, had an inkling of the fact that the spiritual condition has its limitations. If you desire to communicate with those whom you have left, I would strongly advise you to postpone the attempt, and to leave this place, where you will experience only pain and anxiety. Come with me, and learn something of your changed circumstances."

"I am in a dream," said Brenton, "and you are part of it. I went to sleep last night, and am still dreaming. This is a nightmare and it will soon be over."

"You are saying that," said the other, "merely to convince yourself. It is now becoming apparent to you that this is not a dream. If dreams exist, it was a dream which you left, but you have now become awake. If you really think it is a dream, then do as I tell you--come with me and leave it, because you must admit that this part of the dream is at least very unpleasant."

"It is not very pleasant," assented Brenton. As he spoke the bewildered servants came rushing up the stairs, picked up their fallen mistress, and laid her on a sofa. They rubbed her hands and dashed water in her face. She opened her eyes, and then closed them again with a shudder.

"Sarah," she cried, "have I been dreaming, or is your master dead?"

The two girls turned pale at this, and the elder of them went boldly into the room which her mistress had just left. She was evidently a young woman who had herself under good control, but she came out sobbing, with her apron to her eyes.

"Come, come," said the man who stood beside Brenton, "haven't you had enough of this? Come with me; you can return to this house if you wish;" and together they passed out of the room into the crisp air of Christmas morning. But, although Brenton knew it must be cold, he had no feeling of either cold or warmth.

"There are a number of us," said the stranger to Brenton, "who take turns at watching the sick-bed when a man is about to die, and when his spirit leaves his body, we are there to explain, or comfort, or console. Your death was so sudden that we had no warning of it. You did not feel ill before last night, did you?"

"No," replied Brenton. "I felt perfectly well, until after dinner last night."

"Did you leave your affairs in reasonably good order?"

"Yes," said Brenton, trying to recollect. "I think they will find everything perfectly straight."

"Tell me a little of your history, if you do not mind," inquired the other; "it will help me in trying to initiate you into our new order of things here."

"Well," replied Brenton, and he wondered at himself for falling so easily into the other's assumption that he was a dead man, "I was what they call on the earth in reasonably good circumstances. My estate should be worth $100,000. I had $75,000 insurance on my life, and if all that is paid, it should net my widow not far from a couple of hundred thousand."

"How long have you been married?" said the other.

"Only about six months. I was married last July, and we went for a trip abroad. We were married quietly, and left almost immediately afterwards, so we thought, on our return, it would not be a bad plan to give a Christmas Eve dinner, and invite some of our friends. That," he said, hesitating a moment, "was last night. Shortly after dinner, I began to feel rather ill, and went upstairs to rest for a while; and if what you say is true, the first thing I knew I found myself dead."

"Alive," corrected the other.

"Well, alive, though at present I feel I belong more to the world I have left than I do to the world I appear to be in. I must confess, although you are a very plausible gentleman to talk to, that I expect at any moment to wake and find this to have been one of the most horrible nightmares that I ever had the ill luck to encounter."

The other smiled.

"There is very little danger of your waking up, as you call it. Now, I will tell you the great trouble we have with people when they first come to the spirit-land, and that is to induce them to forget entirely the world they have relinquished. Men whose families are in poor circumstances, or men whose affairs are in a disordered state, find it very difficult to keep from trying to set things right again. They have the feeling that they can console or comfort those whom they have left behind them, and it is often a long time before they are convinced that their efforts are entirely futile, as well as very distressing for themselves."

"Is there, then," asked Brenton, "no communication between this world and the one that I have given up?"

The other paused for a moment before he replied.

"I should hardly like to say," he answered, "that there is **no** communication between one world and the other; but the communication that exists is so slight and unsatisfactory, that if you are sensible you will see things with the eyes of those who have very much more experience in this world than you have. Of course, you can go back there as much as you like; there will be no interference and no hindrance.

But when you see things going wrong, when you see a mistake about to be made, it is an appalling thing to stand there helpless, unable to influence those you love, or to point out a palpable error, and convince them that your clearer sight sees it as such. Of course, I understand that it must be very difficult for a man who is newly married, to entirely abandon the one who has loved him, and whom he loves. But I assure you that if you follow the life of one who is as young and handsome as your wife, you will find some one else supplying the consolations you are unable to bestow. Such a mission may lead you to a church where she is married to her second husband. I regret to say that even the most imperturbable spirits are ruffled when such an incident occurs. The wise men are those who appreciate and understand that they are in an entirely new world, with new powers and new limitations, and who govern themselves accordingly from the first, as they will certainly do later on."

"My dear sir," said Brenton, somewhat offended, "if what you say is true, and I am really a dead man----"

"Alive," corrected the other.

"Well, alive, then. I may tell you that my wife's heart is broken. She will never marry again."

"Of course, that is a subject of which you know a great deal more than I do. I all the more strongly advise you never to see her again. It is impossible for you to offer any consolation, and the sight of her grief and misery will only result in unhappiness for yourself. Therefore, take my advice. I have given it very often, and I assure you those who did not take it expressed their regret afterwards. Hold entirely aloof from anything relating to your former life."

Brenton was silent for some moments; finally he said--

"I presume your advice is well meant; but if things are as you state, then I may as well say, first as last, that I do not intend to accept it."

"Very well," said the other; "it is an experience that many prefer to go through for themselves."

"Do you have names in this spirit-land?" asked Brenton, seemingly desirous of changing the subject.

"Yes," was the answer; "we are known by names that we have used in the preparatory school below. My name is Ferris."

"And if I wish to find you here, how do I set about it?"

"The wish is sufficient," answered Ferris. "Merely wish to be with me, and you *are* with me."

"Good gracious!" cried Brenton, "is locomotion so easy as that?"

"Locomotion is very easy. I do not think anything could be easier than it is, and I do not think there could be any improvement in that matter."

"Are there matters here, then, that you think could be improved?"

"As to that I shall not say. Perhaps you will be able to give your own opinion before you have lived here much longer."

"Taking it all in all," said Brenton, "do you think the spirit-land is to be preferred to the one we have left?"

"I like it better," said Ferris, "although I presume there are some who do not. There are many advantages; and then, again, there are many--well, I would not say disadvantages, but still some people consider them such. We are free from the pangs of hunger or cold, and have therefore no need of money, and there is no necessity for the rush and the worry of the world below."

"And how about heaven and hell?" said Brenton. "Are those localities all a myth? Is there nothing of punishment and nothing of reward in this spirit-land?"

There was no answer to this, and when Brenton looked around he found that his companion had departed.

CHAPTER III.

William Brenton pondered long on the situation. He would have known better how to act if he could have been perfectly certain that he was not still the victim of a dream. However, of one thing there was no doubt--namely, that it was particularly harrowing to see what he had seen in his own house. If it were true that he was dead, he said to himself, was not the plan outlined for him by Ferris very much the wiser course to adopt? He stood now in one of the streets of the city so familiar to him. People passed and repassed him--men and women whom he had known in life--but nobody appeared to see him. He resolved, if possible, to solve the problem uppermost in his mind, and learn whether or not he could communicate with an inhabitant of the world he had left. He paused for a moment to consider the best method of doing this. Then he remembered one of his most confidential friends and advisers, and at once wished himself at his office. He found the office closed, but went in to wait for his friend. Occupying the time in thinking over his strange situation, he waited long, and only when the bells began to ring did he remember it was Christmas forenoon, and that his friend would not be at the office that day. The next moment he wished himself at his friend's house, but he was as unsuccessful as at the office; the friend was not at home. The household, however, was in great commotion, and, listening to what was said, he found that the subject of conversation was his own death, and he learned that his friend had gone to the Brenton residence as soon as he heard the startling news of Christmas morning.

Once more Brenton paused, and did not know what to do. He went again into the street. Everything seemed to lead him toward his own home. Although he had told Ferris that he did not intend to take his advice, yet as a sensible man he saw that the admonition was well worth considering, and if he could once become convinced that there was no communication possible between himself and those he had left; if he could give them no comfort and no cheer; if he could see the things which they did not see, and yet be unable to give them warning, he realized that he would merely be adding to his own misery, without alleviating the troubles of others.

He wished he knew where to find Ferris, so that he might have another talk with him. The man impressed him as being exceedingly sensible. No sooner, however, had he wished for the company of Mr. Ferris than he found himself beside that gentleman.

"By George!" he said in astonishment, "you are just the man I wanted to see."

"Exactly," said Ferris; "that is the reason you do see me."

"I have been thinking over what you said," continued the other, "and it strikes me that after all your advice is sensible."

"Thank you," replied Ferris, with something like a smile on his face.

"But there is one thing I want to be perfectly certain about. I want to know whether it is not possible for me to communicate with my friends. Nothing will settle that doubt in my mind except actual experience."

"And have you not had experience enough?" asked Ferris.

"Well," replied the other, hesitating, "I have had some experience, but it seems to me that, if I encounter an old friend, I could somehow make myself felt by him."

"In that case," answered Ferris, "if nothing will convince you but an actual experiment, why don't you go to some of your old friends and try what you can do with them?"

"I have just been to the office and to the residence of one of my old friends. I found at his residence that he had gone to my"--Brenton paused for a moment--"former home. Everything seems to lead me there, and yet, if I take your advice, I must avoid that place of all others."

"I would at present, if I were you," said Ferris. "Still, why not try it with any of the passers-by?"

Brenton looked around him. People were passing and repassing where the two stood talking with each other. "Merry Christmas" was the word on all lips. Finally Brenton said, with a look of uncertainty on his face--

"My dear fellow, I can't talk to any of these people. I don't know them."

Ferris laughed at this, and replied--

"I don't think you will shock them very much; just try it."

"Ah, here's a friend of mine. You wait a moment, and I will accost him." Approaching him, Brenton held out his hand and spoke, but the traveller paid no attention. He passed by as one who had seen or heard nothing.

"I assure you," said Ferris, as he noticed the look of disappointment on the other's face, "you will meet with a similar experience, however much you try. You know the old saying about one not being able to have his cake and eat it too. You can't have the privileges of this world and those of the world you left as well. I think, taking it all in all, you should rest content, although it always hurts those who have left the other world not to be able to communicate with their friends, and at least assure them of their present welfare."

"It does seem to me," replied Brenton, "that would be a great consolation, both for those who are here and those who are left."

"Well, I don't know about that," answered the other. "After all, what does life in the other world amount to? It is merely a preparation for this. It is of so short a space, as compared with the life we live here, that it is hardly worth while to interfere with it one way or another. By the time you are as long here as I have been, you will realize the truth of this."

"Perhaps I shall," said Brenton, with a sigh; "but, meanwhile, what am I to do with myself? I feel like the man who has been all his life in active business, and who suddenly resolves to enjoy himself doing nothing. That sort of thing seems to kill a great number of men, especially if they put off taking a rest until too late, as most of us do."

"Well," said Ferris, "there is no necessity of your being idle here, I assure you. But before you lay out any work for yourself, let me ask you if there is not some interesting part of the world that you would like to visit?"

"Certainly; I have seen very little of the world. That is one of my regrets at leaving it."

"Bless me," said the other, "you haven't left it."

"Why, I thought you said I was a dead man?"

"On the contrary," replied his companion, "I have several times insisted that you have just begun to live. Now where shall we spend the day?"

"How would London do?"

"I don't think it would do; London is apt to be a little gloomy at this time of the year. But what do you say to Naples, or Japan, or, if you don't wish to go out of the United States, Yellowstone Park?"

"Can we reach any of those places before the day is over?" asked Brenton, dubiously.

"Well, I will soon show you how we manage all that. Just wish to accompany me, and I will take you the rest of the way."

"How would Venice do?" said Brenton. "I didn't see half as much of that city as I wanted to."

"Very well," replied his companion, "Venice it is;" and the American city in which they stood faded away from them, and before Brenton could make up his mind exactly what was happening, he found himself walking with his comrade in St. Mark's Square.

"Well, for rapid transit," said Brenton, "this beats anything I've ever had any idea of; but it increases the feeling that I am in a dream."

"You'll soon get used to it," answered Ferris; "and, when you do, the cumbersome methods of travel in the world itself will show themselves in their right light. Hello!" he cried, "here's a man whom I should like you to meet. By the way, I either don't know your name or I have forgotten it."

"William Brenton," answered the other.

"Mr. Speed, I want to introduce you to Mr. Brenton."

"Ah," said Speed, cordially, "a new-comer. One of your victims, Ferris?"

"Say one of his pupils, rather," answered Brenton.

"Well, it is pretty much the same thing," said Speed. "How long have you been with us, and how do you like the country?"

"You see, Mr. Brenton," interrupted Ferris, "John Speed was a newspaper man, and he must ask strangers how they like the country. He has inquired so often while interviewing foreigners for his paper that now he cannot abandon his old phrase. Mr. Brenton has been with us but a short time," continued Ferris, "and so you know, Speed, you can hardly expect him to answer your inevitable question."

"What part of the country are you from?" asked Speed.

"Cincinnati," answered Brenton, feeling almost as if he were an American tourist doing the continent of Europe.

"Cincinnati, eh? Well, I congratulate you. I do not know any place in America that I would sooner die in, as they call it, than Cincinnati. You see, I am a Chicago man myself."

Brenton did not like the jocular familiarity of the newspaper man, and found himself rather astonished to learn that in the spirit-world there were likes and dislikes, just as on earth.

"Chicago is a very enterprising city," he said, in a non-committal way.

"Chicago, my dear sir," said Speed, earnestly, "is *the* city. You will see that Chicago is going to be the great city of the world before you are a hundred years older. By the way, Ferris," said the Chicago man, suddenly recollecting something, "I have got Sommers over here with me."

"Ah!" said Ferris; "doing him any good?"

"Well, precious little, as far as I can see."

"Perhaps it would interest Mr. Brenton to meet him," said Ferris. "I think, Brenton, you asked me a while ago if there was any hell here, or any punishment. Mr. Speed can show you a man in hell."

"Really?" asked Brenton.

"Yes," said Speed; "I think if ever a man was in misery, he is. The trouble with Sommers was this. He--well, he died of delirium tremens, and so, of course, you know what the matter was. Sommers had drunk Chicago whisky for thirty-five years straight along, and never added to it the additional horror of Chicago water. You see what his condition became, both physical and mental. Many people tried to reform Sommers, because he was really a brilliant man; but it was no use. Thirst had become a disease with him, and from the mental part of that disease, although his physical yearning is now gone of course, he suffers. Sommers would give his whole future for one glass of good old Kentucky whisky. He sees it on the counters, he sees men drink it, and he stands beside them in agony. That's why I brought him over here. I thought that he wouldn't see the colour of whisky as it sparkles in the glass; but now he is in the Cafe Quadra watching men drink. You may see him sitting there with all the agony of unsatisfied desire gleaming from his face."

"And what do you do with a man like that?" asked Brenton.

"Do? Well, to tell the truth, there is nothing *to* do. I took him away from Chicago, hoping to ease his trouble a little; but it has had no effect."

"It will come out all right by-and-by," said Ferris, who noticed the pained look on Brenton's face. "It is the period of probation that he has to pass through. It will wear off. He merely goes through the agonies he would have suffered on earth if he had suddenly been deprived of his favourite intoxicant."

"Well," said Speed, "you won't come with me, then? All right, good-bye. I hope to see you again, Mr. Brenton," and with that they separated.

Brenton spent two or three days in Venice, but all the time the old home hunger was upon him. He yearned for news of Cincinnati. He wanted to be back, and several times the wish brought him there, but he instantly returned. At last he said to Ferris--

"I am tired. I must go home. I have *got* to see how things are going."

"I wouldn't if I were you," replied Ferris.

"No, I know you wouldn't. Your temperament is indifferent. I would rather be miserable with knowledge than happy in ignorance. Good-bye."

It was evening when he found himself in Cincinnati. The weather was bright and clear, and apparently cold. Men's feet crisped on the frozen pavement, and the streets had that welcome, familiar look which they always have to the returned traveller when he reaches the city he calls his home. The newsboys were rushing through the streets yelling their papers at the top of their voices. He heard them, but paid little attention.

"All about the murder! Latest edition! All about the poison case!"

He felt that he must have a glimpse at a paper, and, entering the office of an hotel where a man was reading one, he glanced over his shoulder at the page before him, and was horror-stricken to see the words in startling headlines--

THE BRENTON MURDER.

The Autopsy shows that Morphine was the Poison used.
Enough found to have killed a Dozen Men.
Mrs. Brenton arrested for Committing the Horrible
Deed.

CHAPTER IV.

For a moment Brenton was so bewildered and amazed at the awful headlines which he read, that he could hardly realize what had taken place. The fact that he had been poisoned, although it gave him a strange sensation, did not claim his attention as much as might have been thought. Curiously enough he was more shocked at finding himself, as it were, the talk of the town, the central figure of a great newspaper sensation. But the thing that horrified him was the fact that his wife had been arrested for his murder. His first impulse was to go to her at once, but he next thought it better to read what the paper said about the matter, so as to become possessed of all the facts. The headlines, he said to himself, often exaggerated things, and there was a possibility that the body of the article would not bear out the naming announcement above it. But as he read on and on, the situation seemed to become more and more appalling. He saw that his friends had been suspicious of his sudden death, and had insisted on a post-mortem examination. That examination had been conducted by three of the most eminent physicians of Cincinnati, and the three doctors had practically agreed that the deceased, in the language of the verdict, had come to his death through morphia poisoning, and the coroner's jury had brought in a verdict that "the said William Brenton had been poisoned by some person unknown." Then the article went on to state how suspicion had gradually fastened itself upon his wife, and at last her arrest had been ordered. The arrest had taken place that day.

After reading this, Brenton was in an agony of mind. He pictured his dainty and beautiful wife in a stone cell in the city prison. He foresaw the horrors of the public trial, and the deep grief and pain which the newspaper comments on the case would cause to a woman educated and refined. Of course, Brenton had not the slightest doubt in his own mind about the result of the trial. His wife would be triumphantly acquitted; but, all the same, the terrible suspense which she must suffer in the meanwhile would not be compensated for by the final verdict of the jury.

Brenton at once went to the jail, and wandered through that gloomy building, searching for his wife. At last he found her, but it was in a very comfortable room in the sheriffs residence. The terror and the trials of the last few days had aged her perceptibly, and it cut Brenton to the heart to think that he stood there before her, and could not by any means say a soothing word that she would understand. That she had wept many bitter tears since the terrible Christmas morning was evident; there were dark circles under her beautiful eyes that told of sleepless nights. She sat in a comfortable armchair, facing the window; and looked steadily out at the dreary winter scene with eyes that apparently saw nothing. Her hands lay idly on her lap, and now and then she caught her breath in a way that was half a sob and half a gasp.

Presently the sheriff himself entered the room.

"Mrs. Brenton," he said, "there is a gentleman here who wishes to see you. Mr. Roland, he tells me his name is, an old friend of yours. Do you care to see any one?"

The lady turned her head slowly round, and looked at the sheriff for a moment, seemingly not understanding what he said. Finally she answered, dreamily--

"Roland? Oh, Stephen! Yes, I shall be very glad to see him. Ask him to come in, please."

The next moment Stephen Roland entered, and somehow the fact that he had come to console Mrs. Brenton did not at all please the invisible man who stood between them.

"My dear Mrs. Brenton," began Roland, "I hope you are feeling better to-day? Keep up your courage, and be brave. It is only for a very short time. I have retained the noted criminal lawyers, Benham and Brown, for the defence. You could not possibly have better men."

At the word "criminal" Mrs. Brenton shuddered.

"Alice," continued Roland, sitting down near her, and drawing his chair closer to her, "tell me that you will not lose your courage. I want you to be brave, for the sake of your friends."

He took her listless hand in his own, and she did not withdraw it.

Brenton felt passing over him the pangs of impotent rage, as he saw this act on the part of Roland.

Roland had been an unsuccessful suitor for the hand which he now held in his own, and Brenton thought it the worst possible taste, to say the least, that he should take advantage now of her terrible situation to ingratiate himself into her favour.

The nearest approach to a quarrel that Brenton and his wife had had during their short six months of wedded life was on the subject of the man who now held her hand in his own. It made Brenton impatient to think that a woman with all her boasted insight into character, her instincts as to what was right and what was wrong, had such little real intuition that she did not see into the character of the man whom they were discussing; but a woman never thinks it a crime for a man to have been in love with her, whatever opinion of that man her husband may hold.

"It is awful! awful! awful!" murmured the poor lady, as the tears again rose to her eyes.

"Of course it is," said Roland; "it is particularly awful that they should accuse you, of all persons in the world, of this so-called crime. For my part I do not believe that he was poisoned at all, but we will soon straighten things out. Benham and Brown will give up everything and devote their whole attention to this case until it is finished. Everything will be done that money or friends can do, and all that we ask is that you keep up your courage, and do not be downcast with the seeming awfulness of the situation."

Mrs. Brenton wept silently, but made no reply. It was evident, however, that she was consoled by the words and the presence of her visitor. Strange as it may appear, this fact enraged Brenton, although he had gone there for the very purpose of cheering and comforting his wife. All the bitterness he had felt before against his former rival was revived, and his rage was the more agonizing because it was inarticulate. Then there flashed over him Ferris's sinister advice to leave things alone in the world that he had left. He felt that he could stand this no longer, and the next instant he found himself again in the wintry streets of Cincinnati.

The name of the lawyers, Benham and Brown, kept repeating itself in his mind, and he resolved to go to their office and hear, if he could, what preparations were being made for the defence of a woman whom he knew to be innocent. He found, when he got to the office of these noted lawyers, that the two principals were locked in their private room; and going there, he found them discussing the case with the coolness and impersonal feeling that noted lawyers have even when speaking of issues that involve life or death.

"Yes," Benham was saying, "I think that, unless anything new turns up, that is the best line of defence we can adopt."

"What do you think might turn up?" asked Brown.

"Well, you can never tell in these cases. They may find something else--they may find the poison, for instance, or the package that contained it. Perhaps a druggist will remember having sold it to this woman, and then, of course, we shall have to change our plans. I need not say that it is strictly necessary in this case to give out no opinions whatever to newspaper men. The papers will be full of rumours, and it is just as well if we can keep our line of defence hidden until the time for action comes."

"Still," said Brown, who was the younger partner, "it is as well to keep in with the newspaper fellows; they'll be here as soon as they find we have taken charge of the defence."

"Well, I have no doubt you can deal with them in such a way as to give them something to write up, and yet not disclose anything we do not wish known."

"I think you can trust me to do that," said Brown, with a self-satisfied air.

"I shall leave that part of the matter entirely in your hands," replied Benham. "It is better not to duplicate or mix matters, and if any newspaper man comes to see me I will refer him to you. I will say I know nothing of the case whatever."

"Very well," answered Brown. "Now, between ourselves, what do you think of the case?"

"Oh, it will make a great sensation. I think it will probably be one of the most talked-of cases that we have ever been connected with."

"Yes, but what do you think of her guilt or innocence?"

"As to that," said Benham, calmly, "I haven't the slightest doubt. She murdered him."

As he said this, Brenton, forgetting himself for a moment, sprang forward as if to strangle the lawyer. The statement Benham had made seemed the most appalling piece of treachery. That men should take a woman's money for defending her, and actually engage in a case when they believed their client guilty, appeared to Brenton simply infamous.

"I agree with you," said Brown. "Of course she was the only one to benefit by his death. The simple fool willed everything to her, and she knew it; and his doing so is the more astounding when you remember he was quite well aware that she had a former lover whom she would gladly have married if he had been as rich as Brenton. The supreme idiocy of some men as far as their wives are concerned is something awful."

"Yes," answered Benham, "it is. But I tell you, Brown, she is no ordinary woman. The very conception of that murder had a stroke of originality about it that I very much admire. I do not remember anything like it in the annals of crime. It is the true way in which a murder should be committed. The very publicity of the occasion was a safeguard. Think of poisoning a man at a dinner that he has given himself, in the midst of a score of friends. I tell you that there was a dash of bravery about it that commands my admiration."

"Do you imagine Roland had anything to do with it?"

"Well, I had my doubts about that at first, but I think he is innocent, although from what I know of the man he will not hesitate to share the proceeds of the crime. You mark my words, they will be married within a year from now if she is acquitted. I believe Roland knows her to be guilty."

"I thought as much," said Brown, "by his actions here, and by some remarks he let drop. Anyhow, our credit in the affair will be all the greater if we succeed in getting her off. Yes," he continued, rising and pushing back his chair, "Madam Brenton is a murderess."

CHAPTER V.

Brenton found himself once more in the streets of Cincinnati, in a state of mind that can hardly be described. Rage and grief struggled for the mastery, and added to the tumult of these passions was the uncertainty as to what he should do, or what he *could* do. He could hardly ask the advice of Ferris again, for his whole trouble arose from his neglect of the counsel that gentleman had already given him. In his new sphere he did not know where to turn. He found himself wondering whether in the spirit-land there was any firm of lawyers who could advise him, and he remembered then how singularly ignorant he was regarding the conditions of existence in the world to which he now belonged. However, he felt that he must consult with somebody, and Ferris was the only one to whom he could turn. A moment later he was face to face with him.

"Mr. Ferris," he said, "I am in the most grievous trouble, and I come to you in the hope that, if you cannot help me, you can at least advise me what to do."

"If your trouble has come," answered Ferris, with a shade of irony in his voice, "through following the advice that I have already given you, I shall endeavour, as well as I am able, to help you out of it."

"You know very well," cried Brenton, hotly, "that my whole trouble has occurred through neglecting your advice, or, at least, through deliberately not following it. I *could* not follow it."

"Very well, then," said Ferris, "I am not surprised that you are in a difficulty. You must remember that such a crisis is an old story with us here."

"But, my dear sir," said Brenton, "look at the appalling condition of things, the knowledge of which has just come to me. It seems I was poisoned, but of course that doesn't matter. I feel no resentment against the wretch who did it. But the terrible thing is that my wife has been arrested for the crime, and I have just learned that her own lawyers actually believe her guilty."

"That fact," said Ferris, calmly, "will not interfere with their eloquent pleading when the case comes to trial."

Brenton glared at the man who was taking things so coolly, and who proved himself so unsympathetic; but an instant after he realized the futility of quarrelling with the only person who could give him advice, so he continued, with what patience he could command--

"The situation is this: My wife has been arrested for the crime of murdering me. She is now in the custody of the sheriff. Her trouble and anxiety of mind are fearful to contemplate."

"My dear sir," said Ferris, "there is no reason why you or anybody else should contemplate it."

"How can you talk in that cold-blooded way?" cried Brenton, indignantly. "Could you see *your* wife, or any one *you* held dear, incarcerated for a dreadful crime, and yet remain calm and collected, as you now appear to be when you hear of another's misfortune?"

"My dear fellow," said Ferris, "of course it is not to be expected that one who has had so little experience with this existence should have any sense of proportion. You appear to be speaking quite seriously. You do not seem at all to comprehend the utter triviality of all this."

"Good gracious!" cried Brenton, "do you call it a trivial thing that a woman is in danger of her life for a crime which she never committed?"

"If she is innocent," said the other, in no way moved by the indignation of his comrade, "surely that state of things will be brought out in the courts, and no great harm will be done, even looking at things from the standpoint of the world you have left. But I want you to get into the habit of looking at things from the standpoint of this world, and not of the other. Suppose that what you would call the worst should happen--suppose she is hanged--what then?"

Brenton stood simply speechless with indignation at this brutal remark.

"If you will just look at things correctly," continued Ferris, imperturbably, "you will see that there is probably a moment of anguish, perhaps not even that moment, and then your wife is here with you in the land of spirits. I am sure that is a consummation devoutly to be wished. Even a man in your state of mind must see the reasonableness of this. Now, looking at the question in what you would call its most serious aspect, see how little it amounts to. It isn't worth a moment's thought, whichever way it goes."

"You think nothing, then, of the disgrace of such a death--of the bitter injustice of it?"

"When you were in the world did you ever see a child cry over a broken toy? Did the sight pain you to any extent? Did you not know that a new toy could be purchased that would quite obliterate all thoughts of the other? Did the simple griefs of childhood carry any deep and lasting consternation to the mind of a grown-up man? Of course it did not. You are sensible enough to know that. Well, we here in this world look on the pain and struggles and trials of people in the world you have left, just as an aged man looks on the tribulations of children over a broken doll. That is all it really amounts to. That is what I mean when I say that you have not yet got your sense of proportion. Any grief and misery there is in the world you have left is of such an ephemeral, transient nature, that when we think for a moment of the free, untrammelled, and painless life there is beyond, those petty troubles sink into insignificance. My dear fellow, be sensible, take my advice. I have really a strong interest in you, and I advise you, entirely for your own welfare, to forget all about it. Very soon you will have something much more important to do than lingering around the world you have left. If your wife comes amongst us I am sure you will be glad to welcome her, and to teach her the things that you will have already found out of your new life. If she does not appear, then you will know that, even from the old-world standpoint, things have gone what you would call 'all right.' Let these trivial matters go, and attend to the vastly more important concerns that will soon engage your attention here."

Ferris talked earnestly, and it was evident, even to Brenton, that he meant what he said. It was hard to find a pretext for a quarrel with a man at once so calm and so perfectly sure of himself.

"We will not talk any more about it," said Brenton. "I presume people here agree to differ, just as they did in the world we have both left."

"Certainly, certainly," answered Ferris. "Of course, you have just heard my opinion; but you will find myriads of others who do not share it with me. You will meet a great many who are interested in the subject of communication with the world they have left. You will, of course, excuse me when I say that I consider such endeavours not worth talking about."

"Do you know any one who is interested in that sort of thing? and can you give me an introduction to him?"

"Oh! for that matter," said Ferris, "you have had an introduction to one of the most enthusiastic investigators of the subject. I refer to Mr. John Speed, late of Chicago."

"Ah!" said Brenton, rather dubiously. "I must confess that I was not very favourably impressed with Mr. Speed. Probably I did him an injustice."

"You certainly did," said Ferris. "You will find Speed a man well worth knowing, even if he does waste himself on such futile projects as a scheme for communicating with a community so evanescent as that of Chicago. You will like Speed better the more you know him. He really is very philanthropic, and has Sommers on his hands just now. From what he said after you left Venice, I imagine he does not entertain the same feeling toward you as you do toward him. I would see Speed if I were you."

"I will think about it," said Brenton, as they separated.

To know that a man thinks well of a person is no detriment to further acquaintance with that man, even if the first impressions have not been favourable; and after Ferris told Brenton that Speed had thought well of him, Brenton found less difficulty in seeking the Chicago enthusiast.

"I have been in a good deal of trouble," Brenton said to Speed, "and have been talking to Ferris about it. I regret to say that he gave me very little encouragement, and did not seem at all to appreciate my feelings in the matter."

"Oh, you mustn't mind Ferris," said Speed. "He is a first-rate fellow, but he is as cold and unsympathetic as--well, suppose we say as an oyster. His great hobby is non-intercourse with the world we have left. Now, in that I don't agree with him, and there are thousands who don't agree with him. I admit that there are cases where a man is more unhappy if he frequents the old world than he would be if he left it alone. But then there are other cases where just the reverse is true. Take my own experience, for example; I take a peculiar pleasure in rambling around Chicago. I admit that it is a grievance to me, as an old newspaper man, to see the number of scoops I could have on my esteemed contemporaries, but--"

"Scoop? What is that?" asked Brenton, mystified.

"Why, a scoop is a beat, you know."

"Yes, but I don't know. What is a beat?"

"A beat or a scoop, my dear fellow, is the getting of a piece of news that your contemporary does not obtain. You never were in the newspaper business? Well, sir, you missed it. Greatest business in the world. You know everything that is going on long before anybody else does, and the way you can reward your friends and jump with both feet on your enemies is one of the delights of existence down there."

"Well, what I wanted to ask you was this," said Brenton. "You have made a speciality of finding out whether there could be any communication between one of us, for instance, and one who is an inhabitant of the other world. Is such communication possible?"

"I have certainly devoted some time to it, but I can't say that my success has been flattering. My efforts have been mostly in the line of news. I have come on some startling information which my facilities here gave me access to, and I confess I have tried my best to put some of the boys on to it. But there is a link loose somewhere. Now, what is your trouble? Do you want to get a message to anybody?"

"My trouble is this," said Brenton, briefly, "I am here because a few days ago I was poisoned."

"George Washington!" cried the other, "you don't say so! Have the newspapers got on to the fact?"

"I regret to say that they have."

"What an item that would have been if one paper had got hold of it and the others hadn't! I suppose they all got on to it at the same time?"

"About that," said Brenton, "I don't know, and I must confess that I do not care very much. But here is the trouble--my wife has been arrested for my murder, and she is as innocent as I am."

"Sure of that?"

"Sure of it?" cried the other indignantly. "Of course I am sure of it."

"Then who is the guilty person?"

"Ah, that," said Brenton, "I do not yet know."

"Then how can you be sure she is not guilty?"

"If you talk like that," exclaimed Brenton, "I have nothing more to say."

"Now, don't get offended, I beg of you. I am merely looking at this from a newspaper standpoint, you know. You must remember it is not you who will decide the matter, but a jury of your very stupid fellow-countrymen. Now, you can never tell what a jury *will* do, except that it will do something idiotic. Therefore, it seems to me that the very first step to be taken is to find out who the guilty party is. Don't you see the force of that?"

"Yes, I do."

"Very well, then. Now, what were the circumstances of this crime? who was to profit by your death?"

Brenton winced at this.

"I see how it is," said the other, "and I understand why you don't answer. Now--you'll excuse me if I am frank--your wife was the one who benefited most by your death, was she not?"

"No," cried the other indignantly, "she was not the one. That is what the lawyers said. Why in the world should she want to poison me, when she had all my wealth at her command as it was?"

"Yes, that's a strong point," said Speed. "You were a reasonably good husband, I suppose? Rather generous with the cash?"

"Generous?" cried the other. "My wife always had everything she wanted."

"Ah, well, there was no--you'll excuse me, I am sure--no former lover in the case, was there?"

Again Brenton winced, and he thought of Roland sitting beside his wife with her hand in his.

"I see," said Speed; "you needn't answer. Now what were the circumstances, again?"

"They were these: At a dinner which I gave, where some twenty or twenty-five of my friends were assembled, poison, it appears, was put into my cup of coffee. That is all I know of it."

"Who poured out that cup of coffee?"

"My wife did."

"Ah! Now, I don't for a moment say she is guilty, remember; but you must admit that, to a stupid jury, the case *might* look rather bad against her."

"Well, granted that it does, there is all the more need that I should come to her assistance if possible."

"Certainly, certainly!" said Speed. "Now, I'll tell you what we have to do. We must get, if possible, one of the very brightest Chicago reporters on the track of this thing, and we have to get him on the track of it early. Come with me to Chicago. We will try an experiment, and I am sure you will lend your mind entirely to the effort. We must act in conjunction in this affair, and you are just the man I've been wanting, some one who is earnest and who has something at stake in the matter. We may fail entirely, but I think it's worth the trying. Will you come?"

"Certainly," said Brenton; "and I cannot tell you how much I appreciate your interest and sympathy."

Arriving at a brown stone building on the corner of two of the principal streets in Chicago, Brenton and Speed ascended quickly to one of the top floors. It was nearly midnight, and two upper stories of the huge dark building were brilliantly lighted, as was shown on the outside by the long rows of glittering windows. They entered a room where a man was seated at a table, with coat and vest thrown off, and his hat set well back on his head. Cold as it was outside, it was warm in this man's room, and the room was blue with smoke. A black corn-cob pipe was in his teeth, and the man was writing away as if for dear life, on sheets of coarse white copy paper, stopping now and then to fill up his pipe or to relight it after it had gone out.

"There," said Speed, waving his hand towards the writer with a certain air of proprietory pride, "there sits one of the very cleverest men on the Chicago press. That fellow, sir, is gifted with a nose for news which has no equal in America. He will ferret out a case that he once starts on with an unerringness that would charm you. Yes, sir, I got him his present situation on this paper, and I can tell you it was a good one."

"He must have been a warm friend of yours?" said Brenton, indifferently, as if he did not take much interest in the eulogy.

"Quite the contrary," said Speed. "He was a warm enemy, made it mighty warm for *me* sometimes. He was on an opposition paper, but I tell you, although I was no chicken in newspaper business, that man would scoop the daylight out of me any time he tried. So, to get rid of opposition, I got the managing editor to appoint him to a place on our paper; and I tell you, he has never regretted it. Yes, sir, there sits George Stratton, a man who knows his business. Now," he said, "let us concentrate our attention on him. First let us see whether, by putting our whole minds to it, we can make any impression on *his* mind whatever. You see how busily he is engaged. He is thoroughly absorbed in his work. That is George all over. Whatever his assignment is, George throws himself right into it, and thinks of nothing else until it is finished. *Now* then."

In that dingy, well-lighted room George Stratton sat busily pencilling out the lines that were to appear in next morning's paper. He was evidently very much engrossed in his task, as Speed had said. If he had looked about him, which he did not, he would have said that he was entirely alone. All at once his attention seemed to waver, and he passed his hand over his brow, while perplexity came into his face. Then he noticed that his pipe was out, and, knocking the ashes from it by rapping the bowl on the side of the table, he filled it with an absent-mindedness unusual with him. Again he turned to his writing, and again he passed his hand over his brow. Suddenly, without any apparent cause, he looked first to the right and then to the left of him. Once more he tried to write, but, noticing his pipe was out, he struck another match and nervously puffed away, until clouds of blue smoke rose around him. There was a look of annoyance and perplexity in his face as he bent resolutely to his writing. The door opened, and a man appeared on the threshold.

"Anything more about the convention, George?" he said.

"Yes; I am just finishing this. Sort of pen pictures, you know."

"Perhaps you can let me have what you have done. I'll fix it up."

"All right," said Stratton, bunching up the manuscript in front of him, and handing it to the city editor.

That functionary looked at the number of pages, and then at the writer.

"Much more of this, George?" he said. "We'll be a little short of room in the morning, you know."

"Well," said the other, sitting back in his chair, "it is pretty good stuff that. Folks always like the pen pictures of men engaged in the skirmish better than the reports of what most of them say."

"Yes," said the city editor, "that's so."

"Still," said Stratton, "we could cut it off at the last page. Just let me see the last two pages, will you?"

These were handed to him, and, running his eye through them, he drew his knife across one of the pages, and put at the bottom the cabalistic mark which indicated the end of the copy.

"There! I think I will let it go at that. Old Rickenbeck don't amount to much, anyhow. We'll let him go."

"All right," said the city editor. "I think we won't want anything more to-night."

Stratton put his hands behind his head, with his fingers interlaced, and leaned back in his chair, placing his heels upon the table before him. A thought-reader, looking at his face, could almost have followed the theme that occupied his mind. Suddenly bringing his feet down with a crash to the floor, he rose and went into the city editor's room.

"See here," he said. "Have you looked into that Cincinnati case at all?"

"What Cincinnati case?" asked the local editor, looking up.

"Why, that woman who is up for poisoning her husband."

"Oh yes; we had something of it in the despatches this morning. It's rather out of the local line, you know."

"Yes, I know it is. But it isn't out of the paper's line. I tell you that case is going to make a sensation. She's pretty as a picture. Been married only six months, and it seems to be a dead sure thing that she poisoned her husband. That trial's going to make racy reading, especially if they bring in a verdict of guilty."

The city editor looked interested.

"Want to go down there, George?"

"Well, do you know, I think it'll pay."

"Let me see, this is the last day of the convention, isn't it? And Clark comes back from his vacation to-morrow. Well, if you think it's worth it, take a trip down there, and look the ground over, and give us a special article that we can use on the first day of the trial."

"I'll do it," said George.

*   *   *   *   *

Speed looked at Brenton.

"What would old Ferris say *now*, eh?"

CHAPTER VI.

Next morning George Stratton was on the railway train speeding towards Cincinnati. As he handed to the conductor his mileage book, he did not say to him, lightly transposing the old couplet--

"Here, railroad man, take thrice thy fee,   For spirits twain do ride with me."

George Stratton was a practical man, and knew nothing of spirits, except those which were in a small flask in his natty little valise.

When he reached Cincinnati, he made straight for the residence of the sheriff. He felt that his first duty was to become friends with such an important official. Besides this, he wished to have an interview with the prisoner. He had arranged in his mind, on the way there, just how he would write a preliminary article that would whet the appetite of the readers of the Chicago *Argus* for any further developments that might occur during and after the trial. He would write the whole thing in the form of a story. First, there would be a sketch of the life of Mrs. Brenton and her husband. This would be number one, and above it would be the Roman numeral I. Under the heading II. would be a history of the crime. Under III. what had occurred afterwards--the incidents that had led suspicion towards the unfortunate woman, and that sort of thing. Under the numeral IV. would be his interview with the prisoner, if he were fortunate enough to get one. Under V. he would give the general opinion of Cincinnati on the crime, and on the guilt or innocence of Mrs. Brenton. This article he already saw in his mind's eye occupying nearly half a page of the *Argus*. All would be in leaded type, and written in a style and manner that would attract attention, for he felt that he was first on the ground, and would not have the usual rush in preparing his copy which had been the bane of his life. It would give the *Argus* practically the lead in this case, which he was convinced would become one of national importance.

The sheriff received him courteously, and, looking at the card he presented, saw the name Chicago *Argus* in the corner. Then he stood visibly on his guard--an attitude assumed by all wise officials when they find themselves brought face to face with a newspaper man; for they know, however carefully an article may be prepared, it will likely contain some unfortunate overlooked phrase which may have a damaging effect in a future political campaign.

"I wanted to see you," began Stratton, coming straight to the point, "in reference to the Brenton murder."

"I may say at once," replied the sheriff, "that if you wish an interview with the prisoner, it is utterly impossible, because her lawyers, Benham and Brown, have positively forbidden her to see a newspaper man."

"That shows," said Stratton, "they are wise men who understand their business. Nevertheless, I wish to have an interview with Mrs. Brenton. But what I wanted to say to you is this: I believe the case will be very much talked about, and that before many weeks are over. Of course you know the standing the *Argus* has in newspaper circles. What it says will have an influence, even over the Cincinnati press. I think you will admit that. Now a great many newspaper men consider an official their natural enemy. I do not; at least, I do not until I am forced to. Any reference that I may make to you I am more than willing to submit to you before it goes to Chicago. I will give you my word, if you want it, that nothing will be said referring to your official position, or to yourself personally, that you do not see before it appears in print. Of course you will be up for re-election. I never met a sheriff who wasn't."

The sheriff smiled at this, and did not deny it.

"Very well. Now, I may tell you my belief is that this case is going to have a powerful influence on your re-election. Here is a young and pretty woman who is to be tried for a terrible crime. Whether she is guilty or innocent, public sympathy is going to be with her. If I were in your place, I would prefer to be known as her friend rather than as her enemy."

"My dear sir," said the sheriff, "my official position puts me in the attitude of neither friend nor enemy of the unfortunate woman. I have simply a certain duty to do, and that duty I intend to perform."

"Oh, that's all right!" exclaimed the newspaper man, jauntily. "I, for one, am not going to ask you to take a step outside your duties; but an official may do his duty, and yet, at the same time, do a friendly act for a newspaper man, or even for a prisoner. In the language of the old chestnut, 'If you don't help me, don't help the bear.' That's all I ask."

"You maybe sure, Mr. Stratton, that anything I can do to help you I shall be glad to do; and now let me give you a hint. If you want to see Mrs. Brenton, the best thing is to get permission from her lawyers. If I were you I would not see Benham--he's rather a hard nut, Benham is, although you needn't tell him I said so. You get on the right side of Brown. Brown has some political aspirations himself, and he does not want to offend a man on so powerful a paper as the *Argus*, even if it is not a Cincinnati paper. Now, if you make him the same offer you have made to me, I think it will be all right. If he sees your copy before it goes into print, and if you keep your word with him that nothing will appear that he does *not* see, I think you will succeed in getting an interview with Mrs. Brenton. If you bring me a note from Brown, I shall be very glad to allow you to see her."

Stratton thanked the sheriff for his hint. He took down in his note-book the address of the lawyers, and the name especially of Mr. Brown. The two men shook hands, and Stratton felt that they understood each other.

When Mr. Stratton was ushered into the private office of Brown, and handed that gentleman his card, he noticed the lawyer perceptibly freeze over.

"Ahem," said the legal gentleman; "you will excuse me if I say that my time is rather precious. Did you wish to see me professionally?"

"Yes," replied Stratton, "that is, from a newspaper standpoint of the profession."

"Ah," said the other, "in reference to what?"

"To the Brenton case."

"Well, my dear sir, I have had, very reluctantly, to refuse information that I would have been happy to give, if I could, to our own newspaper men; and so I may say to you at once that I scarcely think it will be possible for me to be of any service to an outside paper like the *Argus*"

"Local newspaper men," said Stratton, "represent local fame. That you already possess. I represent national fame, which, if you will excuse my saying so, you do not yet possess. The fact that I am in Cincinnati to-day, instead of in Chicago, shows what we Chicago people think of the Cincinnati case. I believe, and the **Argus** believes, that this case is going to be one of national importance. Now, let me ask you one question. Will you state frankly what your objection is to having a newspaper man, for instance, interview Mrs. Brenton, or get any information relating to this case from her or others whom you have the power of controlling?"

"I shall answer that question," said Brown, "as frankly as you put it. You are a man of the world, and know, of course, that we are all selfish, and in business matters look entirely after our own interests. My interest in this case is to defend my client. Your interest in this case is to make a sensational article. You want to get facts if possible, but, in any event, you want to write up a readable column or two for your paper. Now, if I allowed you to see Mrs. Brenton, she might say something to you, and you might publish it, that would not only endanger her chances, but would seriously embarrass us, as her lawyers, in our defence of the case."

"You have stated the objection very plainly and forcibly," said Stratton, with a look of admiration, as if the powerful arguments of the lawyer had had a great effect on him. "Now, if I understand your argument, it simply amounts to this, that you would have no objection to my interviewing Mrs. Brenton if you have the privilege of editing the copy. In other words, if nothing were printed but what you approve of, you would not have the slightest hesitancy about allowing me that interview."

"No, I don't know that I would," admitted the lawyer.

"Very well, then. Here is my proposition to you: I am here to look after the interests of our paper in this particular case. The **Argus** is probably going to be the first paper outside of Cincinnati that will devote a large amount of space to the Brenton trial, in addition to what is received from the Associated Press dispatches. Now you can give me a great many facilities in this matter if you care to do so, and in return I am perfectly willing to submit to you every line of copy that concerns you or your client before it is sent, and I give you my word of honour that nothing shall appear but what you have seen and approved of. If you want to cut out something that I think is vitally important, then I shall tell you frankly that I intend to print it, but will modify it as much as I possibly can to suit your views."

"I see," said the lawyer. "In other words, as you have just remarked, I am to give you special facilities in this matter, and then, when you find out some fact which I wish kept secret, and which you have obtained because of the facilities I have given to you, you will quite frankly tell me that it must go in, and then, of course, I shall be helpless except to debar you from any further facilities, as you call them. No, sir, I do not care to make any such bargain."

"Well, suppose I strike out that clause of agreement, and say to you that I will send nothing but what you approve of, would you then write me a note to the sheriff and allow me to see the prisoner?"

"I am sorry to say"--the lawyer hesitated for a moment, and glanced at the card, then added--"Mr. Stratton, that I do not see my way clear to granting your request."

"I think," said Stratton, rising, "that you are doing yourself an injustice. You are refusing--I may as well tell you first as last--what is a great privilege. Now, you have had some experience in your business, and I have had some experience in mine, and I beg to inform you that men who are much more prominent in the history of their country than any one I can at present think of in Cincinnati, have tried to balk me in the pursuit of my business, and have failed."

"In that matter, of course," said Brown, "I must take my chances. I don't see the use of prolonging this interview. As you have been so frank as to--I won't say threaten, perhaps warn is the better word--as you have been so good as to warn me, I may, before we part, just give *you* a word of caution. Of course we, in Cincinnati, are perfectly willing to admit that Chicago people are the smartest on earth, but I may say that if you print a word in your paper which is untrue and which is damaging to our side of the case, or if you use any methods that are unlawful in obtaining the information you so much desire, you will certainly get your paper into trouble, and you will run some little personal risk yourself."

"Well, as you remarked a moment ago, Mr. Brown, I shall have to take the chances of that. I am here to get the news, and if I don't succeed it will be the first time in my life."

"Very well, sir," said the lawyer. "I wish you good evening."

"Just one thing more," said the newspaper man, "before I leave you."

"My dear sir," said the lawyer, impatiently, "I am very busy. I've already given you a liberal share of my time. I must request that this interview end at once."

"I thought," said Mr. Stratton, calmly, "that perhaps you might be interested in the first article that I am going to write. I shall devote one column in the *Argus* of the day after to-morrow to your defence of the case, and whether your theory of defence is a tenable one or not."

Mr. Brown pushed back his chair and looked earnestly at the young man. That individual was imperturbably pulling on his gloves, and at the moment was buttoning one of them.

"Our *defence*!" cried the lawyer. "What do you know of our defence?"

"My dear sir," said Stratton, "I know *all* about it."

"Sir, that is impossible. Nobody knows what our defence is to be except Mr. Benham and myself."

"And Mr. Stratton, of the Chicago *Argus*," replied the young man, as he buttoned his coat.

"May I ask, then, what the defence is?"

"Certainly," answered the Chicago man. "Your defence is that Mr. Brenton was insane, and that he committed suicide."

Even Mr. Brown's habitual self-control, acquired by long years of training in keeping his feelings out of sight, for the moment deserted him. He drew his breath sharply, and cast a piercing glance at the young man before him, who was critically watching the lawyer's countenance, although he appeared to be entirely absorbed in buttoning his overcoat. Then Mr. Brown gave a short, dry laugh.

"I have met a bluff before," he said carelessly; "but I should like to know what makes you think that such is our defence?"

"Think!" cried the young man. "I don't think at all; I *know* it."

"How do you know it?"

"Well, for one thing, I know it by your own actions a moment ago. What first gave me an inkling of your defence was that book which is on your table. It is Forbes Winslow on the mind and the brain; a very interesting book, Mr. Brown, *very* interesting indeed. It treats of suicide, and the causes and conditions of the brain that will lead up to it. It is a very good book, indeed, to study in such a case. Good evening, Mr. Brown. I am sorry that we cannot co-operate in this matter."

Stratton turned and walked toward the door, while the lawyer gazed after him with a look of helpless astonishment on his face. As Stratton placed his hand on the door knob, the lawyer seemed to wake up as from a dream.

"Stop!" he cried; "I will give you a letter that will admit you to Mrs. Brenton."

CHAPTER VII.

T here!" said Speed to Brenton, triumphantly, "what do you think of *that*? Didn't I say George Stratton was the brightest newspaper man in Chicago? I tell you, his getting that letter from old Brown was one of the cleverest bits of diplomacy I ever saw. There you had quickness of perception, and nerve. All the time he was talking to old Brown he was just taking that man's measure. See how coolly he acted while he was drawing on his gloves and buttoning his coat as if ready to leave. Flung that at Brown all of a sudden as quiet as if he was saying nothing at all unusual, and all the time watching Brown out of the tail of his eye. Well, sir, I must admit, that although I have known George Stratton for years, I thought he was dished by that Cincinnati lawyer. I thought that George was just gracefully covering up his defeat, and there he upset old Brown's apple-cart in the twinkling of an eye. Now, you see the effect of all this. Brown has practically admitted to him what the line of defence is. Stratton won't publish it, of course; he has promised not to, but you see he can hold that over Brown's head, and get everything he wants unless they change their defence."

"Yes," remarked Brenton, slowly, "he seems to be a very sharp newspaper man indeed; but I don't like the idea of his going to interview my wife."

"Why, what is there wrong about that?"

"Well, there is this wrong about it--that she in her depression may say something that will tell against her."

"Even if she does, what of it? Isn't the lawyer going to see the letter before it is sent to the paper?"

"I am not so sure about that. Do you think Stratton will show the article to Brown if he gets what you call a scoop or a beat?"

"Why, of course he will," answered Speed, indignantly; "hasn't he given him his word that he will?"

"Yes, I know he has," said Brenton, dubiously; "but he is a newspaper man."

"Certainly he is," answered Speed, with strong emphasis; "that is the reason he will keep his word."

"I hope so, I hope so; but I must admit that the more I know you newspaper men, the more I see the great temptation you are under to preserve if possible the sensational features of an article."

"I'll bet you a drink--no, we can't do that," corrected Speed; "but you shall see that, if Brown acts square with Stratton, he will keep his word to the very letter with Brown. There is no use in our talking about the matter here. Let us follow Stratton, and see what comes of the interview."

"I think I prefer to go alone," said Brenton, coldly.

"Oh, as you like, as you like," answered the other, shortly. "I thought you wanted my help in this affair; but if you don't, I am sure I shan't intrude."

"That's all right," said Brenton; "come along. By the way, Speed, what do you think of that line of defence?"

"Well, I don't know enough of the circumstances of the case to know what to think of it. It seems to me rather a good line."

"It can't be a good line when it is not true. It is certain to break down."

"That's so," said Speed; "but I'll bet you four dollars and a half that they'll prove you a raving maniac before they are through with you. They'll show very likely that you tried to poison yourself two or three times; bring on a dozen of your friends to prove that they knew all your life you were insane."

"Do you think they will?" asked Brenton, uneasily.

"Think it? Why, I am sure of it. You'll go down to posterity as one of the most complete lunatics that ever, lived in Cincinnati. Oh, there won't be anything left of you when *they* get through with you."

Meanwhile, Stratton was making his way to the residence of the sheriff.

"Ah," said that official, when they met, "you got your letter, did you? Well, I thought you would."

"If you had heard the conversation between my estimable friend Mr. Brown and myself, up to the very last moment, you wouldn't have thought it."

"Well, Brown is generally very courteous towards newspaper men, and that's one reason you see his name in the papers a great deal."

"If I were a Cincinnati newspaper man, I can assure you that his name wouldn't appear very much in the columns of my paper."

"I am sorry to hear you say that. I thought Brown was very popular with the newspaper men. You got the letter, though, did you?"

"Yes; I got it. Here it is. Read it."

The sheriff scanned the brief note over, and put it in his pocket.

"Just take a chair for a moment, will you, and I will see if Mrs. Brenton is ready to receive you."

Stratton seated himself, and, pulling a paper from his pocket, was busily reading when the sheriff again entered.

"I am sorry to say," he began, "after you have had all this trouble, that Mrs. Brenton positively refuses to see you. You know I cannot *compel* a prisoner to meet any one. You understand that, of course."

"Perfectly," said Stratton, thinking for a moment. "See here, sheriff, I have simply *got* to have a talk with that woman. Now, can't you tell her I knew her husband, or something of that sort? I'll make it all right when I see her."

*   *   *   *   *

"The scoundrel!" said Brenton to Speed, as Stratton made this remark.

"My dear sir," said Speed, "don't you see he is just the man we want? This is not the time to be particular."

"Yes, but think of the treachery and meanness of telling a poor unfortunate woman that he was acquainted with her husband, who is only a few days dead."

"Now, see here," said Speed, "if you are going to look on matters in this way you will be a hindrance and not a help in the affair. Don't you appreciate the situation? Why, Mrs. Brenton's own lawyers, as you have said, think her guilty. What, then, can they learn by talking with her, or what good can they do her with their minds already prejudiced against her? Don't you see that?"

Brenton made no answer to this, but it was evident he was very ill at ease.

*   *   *   *   *

"Did you know her husband?" asked the sheriff.

"No, to tell you the truth, I never heard of him before. But I must see this lady, both for my good and hers, and I am not going to let a little thing like that stand between us. Won't you tell her that I have come with a letter from her own lawyers? Just show her the letter, and say that I will take up but very little of her time. I am sorry to ask this much of you, but you see how I am placed."

"Oh, that's all right," said the sheriff, good-naturedly; "I shall be very glad to do what you wish," and with that he once more disappeared.

The sheriff stayed away longer this time, and Stratton paced the room impatiently. Finally, the official returned, and said--

"Mrs. Brenton has consented to see you. Come this way, please. You will excuse me, I know," continued the sheriff, as they walked along together, "but it is part of my duty to remain in the room while you are talking with Mrs. Brenton."

"Certainly, certainly," said Stratton; "I understand that."

"Very well; then, if I may make a suggestion, I would say this: you should be prepared to ask just what you want to know, and do it all as speedily as possible, for really Mrs. Brenton is in a condition of nervous exhaustion that renders it almost cruel to put her through any rigid cross-examination."

"I understand that also," said Stratton; "but you must remember that she has a very much harder trial to undergo in the future. I am exceedingly anxious to get at the truth of this thing, and so, if it seems to you that I am asking a lot of very unnecessary questions, I hope you will not interfere with me as long as Mrs. Brenton consents to answer."

"I shall not interfere at all," said the sheriff; "I only wanted to caution you, for the lady may break down at any moment. If you can marshal your questions so that the most important ones come first, I think it will be wise. I presume you have them pretty well arranged in your own mind?"

"Well, I can't say that I have; you see, I am entirely in the dark. I got no help whatever from the lawyers, and from what I know of their defence I am thoroughly convinced that they are on the wrong track."

"What! did Brown say anything about the defence? That is not like his usual caution."

"He didn't intend to," answered Stratton; "but I found out all I wanted to know, nevertheless. You see, I shall have to ask what appears to be a lot of rambling, inconsequential questions because you can never tell in a case like this when you may get the key to the whole mystery."

"Well, here we are," said the sheriff, as he knocked at a door, and then pushed it open.

From the moment George Stratton saw Mrs. Brenton his interest in the case ceased to be purely journalistic.

Mrs. Brenton was standing near the window, and she appeared to be very calm and collected, but her fingers twitched nervously, clasping and unclasping each other. Her modest dress of black was certainly a very becoming one.

George thought he had never seen a woman so beautiful.

As she was standing up, she evidently intended the interview to be a short one.

"Madam," said Stratton, "I am very sorry indeed to trouble you; but I have taken a great interest in the solution of this mystery, and I have your lawyers' permission to visit you. I assure you, anything you say will be submitted to them, so that there will be no danger of your case being prejudiced by any statements made."

"I am not afraid," said Mrs. Brenton, "that the truth will injure or prejudice my case."

"I am sure of that," answered the newspaper man; and then, knowing that she would not sit down if he asked her to, he continued diplomatically, "Madam, will you permit me to sit down? I wish to write out my notes as carefully as possible. Accuracy is my strong point."

"Certainly," said Mrs. Brenton; and, seeing that it was not probable the interview would be a short one, she seated herself by the window, while the sheriff took a chair in the corner, and drew a newspaper from his pocket.

"Now, madam," said the special, "a great number of the questions I ask you may seem trivial, but as I said to the sheriff a moment ago, some word of yours that appears to you entirely unconnected with the case may give me a clue which will be exceedingly valuable. You will, therefore, I am sure, pardon me if some of the questions I ask you appear irrelevant."

Mrs. Brenton bowed her head, but said nothing.

"Were your husband's business affairs in good condition at the time of his death?"

"As far as I know they were."

"Did you ever see anything in your husband's actions that would lead you to think him a man who might have contemplated suicide?"

Mrs. Brenton looked up with wide-open eyes.

"Certainly not," she said.

"Had he ever spoken to you on the subject of suicide?"

"I do not remember that he ever did."

"Was he ever queer in his actions? In short, did you ever notice anything about him that would lead you to doubt his sanity? I am sorry if questions I ask you seem painful, but I have reasons for wishing to be certain on this point."

"No," said Mrs. Brenton; "he was perfectly sane. No man could have been more so. I am certain that he never thought of committing suicide."

"Why are you so certain on that point?"

"I do not know why. I only know I am positive of it."

"Do you know if he had any enemy who might wish his death?"

"I doubt if he had an enemy in the world. I do not know of any."

"Have you ever heard him speak of anybody in a spirit of enmity?"

"Never. He was not a man who bore enmity against people. Persons whom he did not like he avoided."

"The poison, it is said, was put into his cup of coffee. Do you happen to know," said Stratton, turning to the sheriff, "how they came to that conclusion?"

"No, I do not," answered the sheriff. "In fact, I don't see any reason why they should think so."

"Was morphia found in the coffee cup afterwards?"

"No; at the time of the inquest all the things had been cleared away. I think it was merely presumed that the morphine was put into his coffee."

"Who poured out the coffee he drank that night?"

"I did," answered his wife.

"You were at one end of the table and he at the other, I suppose?"

"Yes."

"How did the coffee cup reach him?"

"I gave it to the servant, and she placed it before him."

"It passed through no other hands, then?"

"No."

"Who was the servant?"

Mrs. Brenton pondered for a moment.

"I really know very little about her. She had been in our house for a couple of weeks only."

"What was her name?"

"Jane Morton, I think."

"Where is she now, do you know?"

"I do not know."

"She appeared at the inquest, of course?" said Stratton, turning to the sheriff.

"I think she did," was the answer. "I am not sure."

He marked her name down in the note-book.

"How many people were there at the dinner?"

"Including my husband and myself, there were twenty-six."

"Could you give me the name of each of them?"

"Yes, I think so."

She repeated the names, which he took down, with certain notes and comments on each.

"Who sat next your husband at the head of the table?"

"Miss Walker was at his right hand, Mr. Roland at his left."

"Now, forgive me if I ask you if you have ever had any trouble with your husband?"

"Never."

"Never had any quarrel?"

Mrs. Brenton hesitated for a moment.

"No, I don't think we ever had what could be called a quarrel."

"You had no disagreement shortly before the dinner?"

Again Mrs. Brenton hesitated.

"I can hardly call it a disagreement," she said. "We had a little discussion about some of the guests who were to be invited."

"Did he object to any that were there?"

"There was a gentleman there whom he did not particularly like, I think, but he made no objection to his coming; in fact, he seemed to feel that I might imagine he had an objection from a little discussion we had about inviting him; and afterwards, as if to make up for that, he placed this guest at his left hand."

Stratton quickly glanced up the page of his notebook, and marked a little cross before the name of Stephen Roland.

"You had another disagreement with him before, if I might term it so, had you not?"

Mrs. Brenton looked at him surprised.

"What makes you think so?" she said.

"Because you hesitated when I spoke of it."

"Well, we had what you might call a disagreement once at Lucerne, Switzerland."

"Will you tell me what it was about?"

"I would rather not."

"Will you tell me this--was it about a gentleman?"

"Yes," said Mrs. Brenton.

"Was your husband of a jealous disposition?"

"Ordinarily I do not think he was. It seemed to me at the time that he was a little unjust--that's all."

"Was the gentleman in Lucerne?"

"Oh no!"

"In Cincinnati?"

"Yes."

"Was his name Stephen Roland?"

Mrs. Brenton again glanced quickly at the newspaper man, and seemed about to say something, but, checking herself, she simply answered--

"Yes."

Then she leaned back in the armchair and sighed.

"I am very tired," she said. "If it is not absolutely necessary, I prefer not to continue this conversation."

Stratton immediately rose.

"Madam," he said, "I am very much obliged to you for the trouble you have taken to answer my questions, which I am afraid must have seemed impertinent to you, but I assure you that I did not intend them to be so. Now, madam, I would like very much to get a promise from you. I wish that you would promise to see me if I call again, and I, on my part, assure you that unless I have something particularly important to tell you, or to ask, I shall not intrude upon you."

"I shall be pleased to see you at any time, sir."

When the sheriff and the newspaper man reached the other room, the former said--

"Well, what do you think?"

"I think it is an interesting case," was the answer.

"Or, to put it in other words, you think Mrs. Brenton a very interesting lady."

"Officially, sir, you have exactly stated my opinion."

"And I suppose, poor woman, she will furnish an interesting article for the paper?"

"Hang the paper!" said Stratton, with more than his usual vim.

The sheriff laughed. Then he said--

"I confess that to me it seems a very perplexing affair all through. Have you got any light on the subject?"

"My dear sir, I will tell you three important things. First, Mrs. Brenton is innocent. Second, her lawyers are taking the wrong line of defence. Third," tapping his breast-pocket, "I have the name of the murderer in my note-book."

CHAPTER VIII.

N ow," said John Speed to William Brenton, "we have got Stratton fairly started on the track, and I believe that he will ferret out the truth in this matter. But, meanwhile, we must not be idle. You must remember that, with all our facilities for discovery, we really know nothing of the murderer ourselves. I propose we set about this thing just as systematically as Stratton will. The chances are that we shall penetrate the mystery of the whole affair very much quicker than he. As I told you before, I am something of a newspaper man myself; and if, with the facilities of getting into any room in any house, in any city and in any country, and being with a suspected criminal night and day when he never imagines any one is near him--if with all those advantages I cannot discover the real author of that crime before George Stratton does, then I'll never admit that I came from Chicago, or belonged to a newspaper."

"Whom do you think Stratton suspects of the crime? He told the sheriff," said Brenton, "that he had the name in his pocket-book."

"I don't know," said Speed, "but I have my suspicions. You see, he has the names of all the guests at your banquet in that pocket-book of his; but the name of Stephen Roland he has marked with two crosses. The name of the servant he has marked with one cross. Now, I suspect that he believes Stephen Roland committed the crime. You know Roland; what do you think of him?"

"I think he is quite capable of it," answered Brenton, with a frown.

"Still, you are prejudiced against the man," put in Speed, "so your evidence is hardly impartial."

"I am not prejudiced against any one," answered Brenton; "I merely know that man. He is a thoroughly despicable, cowardly character. The only thing that makes me think he would not commit a murder, is that he is too craven to stand the consequences if he were caught. He is a cool villain, but he is a coward. I do not believe he has the courage to commit a crime, even if he thought he would benefit by it."

"Well, there is one thing, Brenton, you can't be accused of flattering a man, and if it is any consolation for you to know, you may be pretty certain that George Stratton is on his track."

"I am sure I wish him success," answered Brenton, gloomily; "if he brings Roland to the gallows I shall not mourn over it."

"That's all right," said Speed; "but now we must be up and doing ourselves. Have you anything to propose?"

"No, I have not, except that we might play the detective on Roland."

"Well, the trouble with that is we would merely be duplicating what Stratton is doing himself. Now, I'll tell you my proposal. Supposing that we consult with Lecocq."

"Who is that? The novelist?"

"Novelist? I don't think he has ever written any novels--not that I remember of."

"Ah, I didn't know. It seemed to me that I remembered his name in connection with some novel."

"Oh, very likely you did. He is the hero of more detective stories than any other man I know of. He was the great French detective."

"What, is he dead, then?"

"Dead? Not a bit of it; he's here with us. Oh, I understand what you mean. Yes, from your point of view, he is dead."

"Where can we find him?"

"Well, I presume, in Paris. He's a first-rate fellow to know, anyhow, and he spends most of his time around his old haunts. In fact, if you want to be certain to find Lecocq, you will generally get him during office hours in the room he used to frequent while in Paris."

"Let us go and see him, then."

*　　*　　*　　*　　*

"Monsieur Lecocq," said Speed, a moment afterwards, "I wish to introduce to you a new-comer, Mr. Brenton, recently of Cincinnati."

"Ah, my dear Speed," said the Frenchman, "I am very pleased indeed to meet any friend of yours. How is the great Chicago, the second Paris, and how is your circulation?--the greatest in the world, I suppose."

"Well, it is in pretty good order," said Speed; "we circulated from Chicago to Paris here in a very much shorter time than the journey usually occupies down below. Now, can you give us a little of your time? Are you busy just now?"

"My dear Speed, I am always busy. I am like the people of the second Paris. I lose no time, but I have always time to speak with my friends."

"All right," said Speed. "I am like the people of the second Chicago, generally more intent on pleasure than business; but, nevertheless, I have a piece of business for you."

"The second Chicago?" asked Lecocq. "And where is that, pray?"

"Why, Paris, of course," said Speed.

Lecocq laughed.

"You are incorrigible, you Chicagoans. And what is the piece of business?"

"It is the old thing, monsieur. A mystery to be unravelled. Mr. Brenton here wishes to retain you in his case."

"And what is his case?" was the answer.

Lecocq was evidently pleased to have a bit of real work given him.

Speed briefly recited the facts, Brenton correcting him now and then on little points where he was wrong. Speed seemed to think these points immaterial, but Lecocq said that attention to trivialities was the whole secret of the detective business.

"Ah," said Lecocq, sorrowfully, "there is no real trouble in elucidating that mystery. I hoped it would be something difficult; but, you see, with my experience of the old world, and with the privileges one enjoys in this world, things which might be difficult to one below are very easy for us. Now, I shall show you how simple it is."

"Good gracious!" cried Speed, "you don't mean to say you are going to read it right off the reel, like that, when we have been bothering ourselves with it so long, and without success?"

"At the moment," replied the French detective, "I am not prepared to say who committed the deed. That is a matter of detail. Now, let us see what we know, and arrive, from that, at what we do not know. The one fact, of which we are assured on the statement of two physicians from Cincinnati, is that Mr. Brenton was poisoned."

"Well," said Speed, "there are several other facts, too. Another fact is that Mrs. Brenton is accused of the crime."

"Ah! my dear sir," said Lecocq, "that is not pertinent."

"No," said Speed, "I agree with you. I call it very impertinent."

Brenton frowned, at this, and his old dislike to the flippant Chicago man rose to the surface again.

The Frenchman continued marking the points on his long forefinger.

"Now, there are two ways by which that result may have been attained. First, Mr. Brenton may have administered to himself the poison; secondly, the poison may have been administered by some one else."

"Yes," said Speed; "and, thirdly, the poison may have been administered accidentally--you do not seem to take that into account."

"I do not take that into account," calmly replied the Frenchman, "because of its improbability. If there were an accident; if, for instance, the poison was in the sugar, or in some of the viands served, then others than Mr. Brenton would have been poisoned. The fact that one man out of twenty-six was poisoned, and the fact that several people are to benefit by his death, point, it seems to me, to murder; but to be sure of that, I will ask Mr. Brenton one question. My dear sir, did you administer this poison to yourself?"

"Certainly not," answered Brenton.

"Then we have two facts. First, Mr. Brenton was poisoned; secondly, he was poisoned by some person who had an interest in his death. Now we will proceed. When Mr. Brenton sat down to that dinner he was perfectly well. When he arose from that dinner he was feeling ill. He goes to bed. He sees no one but his wife after he has left the dinner-table, and he takes nothing between the time he leaves the dinner-table and the moment he becomes unconscious. Now, that poison must have been administered to Mr. Brenton at the dinner-table. Am I not right?"

"Well, you seem to be," answered Speed.

"Seem? Why, it is as plain as day. There cannot be any mistake."

"All right," said Speed; "go ahead. What next?"

"What next? There were twenty-six people around that table, with two servants to wait on them, making twenty-eight in all. There were twenty-six, I think you said, including Mr. Brenton."

"That is correct."

"Very well. One of those twenty-seven persons has poisoned Mr. Brenton. Do you follow me?"

"We do," answered Speed; "we follow you as closely as you have ever followed a criminal! Go on."

"Very well, so much is clear. These are all facts, not theories. Now, what is the thing that I should do if I were in Cincinnati? I would find out whether one or more of those guests had anything to gain by the death of their host. That done, I would follow the suspected persons. I would have my men find out what each of them had done for a month before the time of the crime. Whoever committed it made some preparation. He did something, too, as you say, in America, to cover up his tracks. Very well. By the keen detective these actions are easily traced. I shall at once place twenty-seven of the best men I know on the track of those twenty-seven persons."

"I call that shadowing with a vengeance," remarked the Chicago man.

"It will be very easy. The one who has committed the crime is certain, when he is alone in his own room, to say something, or to do something, that will show my detective that he is the criminal. So, gentlemen, if you can tell me who those twenty-seven persons are, in three days or a week from this time I will tell you who gave the poison to Mr. Brenton."

"You seem very sure of that," said Speed.

"Sure of it? It is simply child's play. It is mere waiting. If, for instance, at the trial Mrs. Brenton is found guilty, and sentenced, the one who is the guilty party is certain to betray himself or herself as soon as he or she is alone. If it be a man who hopes to marry Mrs. Brenton, he will be overcome with grief at what has happened. He will wring his hands and try to think what can be done to prevent the sentence being carried out. He will argue with himself whether it is better to give himself up and tell the truth, and if he is a coward he will conclude not to do that, but will try to get a pardon, or at least have the capital sentence commuted into life imprisonment. He will possibly be cool and calm in public, but when he enters his own room, when his door is locked, when he believes no one can see him, when he thinks he is alone, then will come his trial. Then his passions and his emotions will betray him. It is mere child's play, as I tell you, and long before there is a verdict I will give you the name of the murderer."

"Very well, then," said Speed, "that is agreed; we will look you up in a week from now."

"I should be pained," said Lecocq, "to put you to that trouble. As soon as I get the report from my men I will communicate with you and let you know the result. In a few days I shall give you the name of the assassin."

"Good-bye, then, until I see you again," answered Speed; and with this he and Brenton took their departure.

"He seems to be very sure of himself," said Brenton.

"He will do what he says, you may depend on that."

The week was not yet up when Monsieur Lecocq met John Speed in Chicago.

"By the look of satisfaction on your face," said Mr. Speed, "I imagine you have succeeded in unravelling the mystery."

"Ah," replied the Frenchman; "if I have the appearance of satisfaction, it is indeed misplaced."

"Then you have not made any discovery?"

"On the contrary, it is all as plain as your big buildings here. It is not for that reason, but because it is so simple that I should be foolish to feel satisfaction regarding it."

"Then who is the person?"

"The assassin," replied the Frenchman, "is one whom no one has seemed to think of, and yet one on whom suspicion should have been the first to fall. The person who did Monsieur Brenton the honour to poison him is none other than the servant girl, Jane Morton."

CHAPTER IX.

J ane Morton!" cried Speed; "who is she?"

"She is, as you may remember, the girl who carried the coffee from Mrs. Brenton to monsieur."

"And are you sure she is the criminal?"

The great detective did not answer; he merely gave an expressive little French gesture, as though the question was not worth commenting upon.

"Why, what was her motive?" asked Speed.

For the first time in their acquaintance a shade of perplexity seemed to come over the enthusiastic face of the volatile Frenchman.

"You are what you call smart, you Chicago people," he said, "and you have in a moment struck the only point on which we are at a loss."

"My dear sir," returned Speed, "that is *the* point in the case. Motive is the first thing to look for, it seems to me. You said as much yourself. If you haven't succeeded in finding what motive Jane Morton had for poisoning her employer, it appears to me that very little has been accomplished."

"Ah, you say that before you know the particulars. I am certain we shall find the motive. What I know now is that Jane Morton is the one who put the poison in his cup of coffee."

"It would take a good deal of nerve to do that with twenty-six people around the table. You forget, my dear sir, that she had to pass the whole length of the table, after taking the cup, before giving it to Mr. Brenton."

"Half of the people had their backs to her, and the other half, I can assure you, were not looking at her. If the poison was ready, it was a very easy thing to slip it into a cup of coffee. There was ample time to do it, and that is how it was done."

"May I ask how you arrived at that conclusion?"

"Certainly, certainly, my dear sir. My detectives report that each one of the twenty-seven people they had to follow were shadowed night and day. But only two of them acted suspiciously. These two were Jane Morton and Stephen Roland. Stephen Roland's anxiety is accounted for by the fact that he is evidently in love with Mrs. Brenton. But the change in Jane Morton has been something terrible. She is suffering from the severest pangs of ineffectual remorse. She has not gone out again to service, but occupies a room in one of the poorer quarters of the city--a room that she never leaves except at night. Her whole actions show that she is afraid of the police--afraid of being tracked for her crime. She buys a newspaper every night, locks and bars the door on entering her room, and, with tears streaming from her eyes, reads every word of the criminal news. One night, when she went out to buy her paper, and what food she needed for the next day, she came unexpectedly upon a policeman at the corner. The man was not looking at her at all, nor for her, but she fled, running like a deer, doubling and turning through alleys and back streets until by a very roundabout road she reached her own room. There she locked herself in, and remained without food all next day rather than go out again. She flung herself terror-stricken on the bed, after her room door was bolted, and cried, 'Oh, why did I do it? why did I do it? I shall certainly be found out. If Mrs. Brenton is acquitted, they will be after me next day. I did it to make up to John what he had suffered, and yet if John knew it, he would never speak to me again.'"

"Who is John?" asked Speed.

"Ah, that," said the detective, "I do not know. When we find out who John is, then we shall find the motive for the crime."

"In that case, if I were you, I should try to find John as quickly as possible."

"Yes, my dear sir, that is exactly what should be done, and my detective is now endeavouring to discover the identity of John. He will possibly succeed in a few days. But there is another way of finding out who John is, and perhaps in that you can help me."

"What other way?"

"There is one man who undoubtedly knows who John is, and that is Mr. Brenton. Now, I thought that perhaps you, who know Brenton better than I do, would not mind asking him who John is."

"My dear sir," said Speed, "Brenton is no particular friend of mine, and I only know him well enough to feel that if there is any cross-examination to be done, I should prefer somebody else to do it."

"Why, you are not afraid of him, are you?" asked the detective.

"Afraid of him? Certainly not, but I tell you that Brenton is just a little touchy and apt to take offence. I have found him so on several occasions. Now, as you have practically taken charge of this case, why don't you go and see him?"

"I suppose I shall have to do that," said the Frenchman, "if you will not undertake it."

"No, I will not."

"You have no objection, have you, to going with me?"

"It is better for you to see Brenton alone. I do not think he would care to be cross-examined before witnesses, you know."

"Ah, then, good-bye; I shall find out from Mr. Brenton who John is."

"I am sure I wish you luck," replied Speed, as Lecocq took his departure.

Lecocq found Brenton and Ferris together. The cynical spirit seemed to have been rather sceptical about the accounts given him of the influence that Speed and Brenton, combined, had had upon the Chicago newspaper man. Yet he was interested in the case, and although he still maintained that no practical good would result, even if a channel of communication could be opened between the two states of existence, he had listened with his customary respect to what Brenton had to say.

"Ah," said Brenton, when he saw the Frenchman, "have you any news for me?"

"Yes, I have. I have news that I will exchange, but meanwhile I want some news from you."

"I have none to give you," answered Brenton.

"If you have not, will you undertake to answer any questions I shall ask you, and not take offence if the questions seem to be personal ones?"

"Certainly," said Brenton; "I shall be glad to answer anything as long as it has a bearing on the case."

"Very well, then, it has a very distinct bearing on the case. Do you remember the girl Jane Morton?"

"I remember her, of course, as one of the servants in our employ. I know very little about her, though."

"That is just what I wish to find out. Do you know *anything* about her?"

"No; she had been in our employ but a fortnight, I think, or perhaps it was a month. My wife attended to these details, of course. I knew the girl was there, that is all."

The Frenchman looked very dubious as Brenton said this, while the latter rather bridled up.

"You evidently do not believe me?" he cried.

Once more the detective gave his customary gesture, and said--

"Ah, pardon me, you are entirely mistaken. I have this to acquaint you with. Jane Morton is the one who murdered you. She did it, she says, partly for the sake of John, whoever he is, and partly out of revenge. Now, of course, you are the only man who can give me information as to the motive. That girl certainly had a motive, and I should like to find out what the motive was."

Brenton meditated for a few moments, and then suddenly brightened up.

"I remember, now, an incident which happened a week of two before Christmas, which may have a bearing on the case. One night I heard--or thought I heard--a movement downstairs, when I supposed everybody had retired. I took a revolver in my hand, and went cautiously down the stairs. Of course I had no light, because, if there was a burglar, I did not wish to make myself too conspicuous a mark. As I went along the hall leading to the kitchen, I saw there was a light inside; but as soon as they heard me coming the light was put out. When I reached the kitchen, I noticed a man trying to escape through the door that led to the coalshed. I fired at him twice, and he sank to the floor with a groan. I thought I had bagged a burglar sure, but it turned out to be nothing of the kind. He was merely a young man who had been rather late visiting one of the girls. I suspect now the girl he came to see was Jane Morton. As it was, the noise brought the two girls there, and I never investigated the matter or tried to find out which one it was that he had been visiting. They were both terror-stricken, and the young man himself was in a state of great fear. He thought for a moment that he had been killed. However, he was only shot in the leg, and I sent him to the house of a physician who keeps such patients as do not wish to go to the hospital. I did not care to have him go to the hospital, because I was afraid the newspapers would get hold of the incident, and make a sensation of it. The whole thing was accidental; the young fellow realized that, and so, I thought, did the girls; at least, I never noticed anything in their behaviour to show the contrary."

"What sort of a looking girl is Jane Morton?" asked Ferris.

"She is a tall brunette, with snapping black eyes."

"Ah, then, I remember her going into the room where you lay," said Ferris, "on Christmas morning. It struck me when she came out that she was very cool and self-possessed, and not at all surprised."

"All I can say," said Brenton, "is that I never noticed anything in her conduct like resentment at what had happened. I intended to give the young fellow a handsome compensation for his injury, but of course what occurred on Christmas Eve prevented that: I had really forgotten all about the circumstance, or I should have told you of it before."

"Then," said Lecocq, "the thing now is perfectly clear. That black-eyed vixen murdered you out of revenge."

CHAPTER X.

It was evident to George Stratton that he would have no time before the trial came off in which to prove Stephen Roland the guilty person. Besides this, he was in a strange state of mind which he himself could not understand. The moment he sat down to think out a plan by which he could run down the man he was confident had committed the crime, a strange wavering of mind came over him. Something seemed to say to him that he was on the wrong track. This became so persistent that George was bewildered, and seriously questioned his own sanity. Whenever he sat alone in his own room, the doubts arose and a feeling that he was on the wrong scent took possession of him. This feeling became so strong at times that he looked up other clues, and at one time tried to find out the whereabouts of the servant girls who had been employed by the Brentons. Curiously enough, the moment he began this search, his mind seemed to become clearer and easier; and when that happened, the old belief in the guilt of Stephen Roland resumed its sway again. But the instant he tried to follow up what clues he had in that direction, he found himself baffled and assailed again by doubts, and so every effort he put forth appeared to be nullified. This state of mind was so unusual with him that he had serious thoughts of abandoning the whole case and going back to Chicago. He said to himself, "I am in love with this woman and I shall go crazy if I stay here any longer." Then he remembered the trust she appeared to have in his powers of ferreting out the mystery of the case, and this in turn encouraged him and urged him on.

All trace of the girls appeared to be lost. He hesitated to employ a Cincinnati detective, fearing that what he discovered would be given away to the Cincinnati press. Then he accused himself of disloyalty to Mrs. Brenton, in putting his newspaper duty before his duty to her. He was so torn by his conflicting ideas and emotions that at last he resolved to abandon the case altogether and return to Chicago. He packed up his valise and resolved to leave that night for big city, trial or no trial. He had described his symptoms to a prominent physician, and that physician told him that the case was driving him mad, and the best thing he could do was to leave at once for other scenes. He could do no good, and would perhaps end by going insane himself.

As George Stratton was packing his valise in his room, alone, as he thought, the following conversation was taking place beside him.

"It is no use," said Speed; "we are merely muddling him, and not doing any good. The only thing is to leave him alone. If he investigates the Roland part of the case he will soon find out for himself that he is on the wrong track; then he will take the right one."

"Yes," said Brenton; "but the case comes on in a few days. If anything is to be done, it must be done now."

"In that I do not agree with you," said Speed. "Perhaps everything will go all right at the trial, but even if it does not, there is still a certain amount of time. You see how we have spoiled things by interfering. Our first success with him has misled us. We thought we could do anything; we have really done worse than nothing, because all this valuable time has been lost. If he had been allowed to proceed in his own way he would have ferreted out the matter as far as Stephen Roland is concerned, and would have found that there was no cause for his suspicion. As it is he has done nothing. He still believes, if left alone, that Stephen Roland is the criminal. All our efforts to lead him to the residence of Jane Morton have been unavailing. Now, you see, he is on the eve of going back to Chicago."

"Well, then, let him go," said Brenton, despondently.

"With all my heart, say I," answered Speed; "but in any case let us leave him alone."

Before the train started that night Stratton said to himself that he was a new man. Richard was himself again. He was thoroughly convinced of the guilt of Stephen Roland, and wondered why he had allowed his mind to wander off the topic and waste time with other suspicions, for which he now saw there was no real excuse. He had not the time, he felt, to investigate the subject personally, but he flattered himself he knew exactly the man to put on Roland's track, and, instead of going himself to Chicago, he sent off the following despatch:--

"Meet me to-morrow morning, without fail, at the Gibson House. Answer."

Before midnight he had his answer, and next morning he met a man in whom he had the most implicit confidence, and who had, as he said, the rare and valuable gift of keeping his mouth shut.

"You see this portrait?" Stratton said, handing to the other a photograph of Stephen Roland. "Now, I do not know how many hundred chemist shops there are in Cincinnati, but I want you to get a list of them, and you must not omit the most obscure shop in town. I want you to visit every drug store there is in the city, show this photograph to the proprietor and the clerks, and find out if that man bought any chemicals during the week or two preceding Christmas. Find out what drugs he bought, and where he bought them, then bring the information to me."

"How much time do you give me on this, Mr. Stratton?" was the question.

"Whatever time you want. I wish the thing done thoroughly and completely, and, as you know, silence is golden in a case like this."

"Enough said," replied the other, and, buttoning the photograph in his inside pocket, he left the room.

* * * * *

There is no necessity of giving an elaborate report of the trial. Any one who has curiosity in the matter can find the full particulars from the files of any paper in the country. Mrs. Brenton was very pale as she sat in the prisoner's dock, but George Stratton thought he never saw any one look so beautiful. It seemed to him that any man in that crowded courtroom could tell in a moment that she was not guilty of the crime with which she was charged, and he looked at the jury of twelve supposedly good men, and wondered what they thought of it.

The defence claimed that it was not their place to show who committed the murder. That rested with the prosecution. The prosecution, Mr. Benham maintained, had signally failed to do this. However, in order to aid the prosecution, he was quite willing to show how Mr. Brenton came to his death. Then witnesses were called, who, to the astonishment of Mrs. Brenton, testified that her husband had all along had a tendency to insanity. It was proved conclusively that some of his ancestors had died in a lunatic asylum, and one was stated to have committed suicide. The defence produced certain books from Mr. Brenton's library, among them Forbes Winslow's volume on "The Mind and the Brain," to show that Brenton had studied the subject of suicide.

The judge's charge was very colourless. It amounted simply to this: If the jury thought the prosecution had shown Mrs. Brenton to have committed the crime, they were to bring in a verdict of guilty, and if they thought otherwise they were to acquit her; and so the jury retired.

As they left the court-room a certain gloom fell upon all those who were friendly to the fair prisoner.

Despite the great reputation of Benham and Brown, it was the thought of every one present that they had made a very poor defence. The prosecution, on the other hand, had been most ably conducted. It had been shown that Mrs. Brenton was chiefly to profit by her husband's death. The insurance fund alone would add seventy-five thousand dollars to the money she would control. A number of little points that Stratton had given no heed to had been magnified, and appeared then to have a great bearing on the case. For the first time, Stratton admitted to himself that the prosecution had made out a very strong case of circumstantial evidence. The defence, too, had been so deplorably weak that it added really to the strength of the prosecution. A great speech had been expected of Benham, but he did not rise to the occasion, and, as one who knew him said, Benham evidently believed his client guilty.

As the jury retired, every one in the court-room felt that there was little hope for the prisoner; and this feeling was intensified when, a few moments after, the announcement was made in court, just as the judge was preparing to leave the bench, that the jury had agreed on the verdict.

Stratton, in the stillness of the court-room, heard one lawyer whisper to another, "She's doomed."

There was intense silence as the jury slowly filed into their places, and the foreman stood up.

"Gentlemen of the jury," was the question, "have you agreed upon a verdict?"

"We have," answered the foreman.

"Do you find the prisoner guilty or not guilty?"

"Not guilty," was the clear answer.

At this there was first a moment of silence, and then a ripple of applause, promptly checked.

Mrs. Brenton was free.

CHAPTER XI.

George Stratton sat in the court-room for a moment dazed, before he thought of the principal figure in the trial; then he rose to go to her side, but he found that Roland was there before him. He heard her say, "Get me a carriage quickly, and take me away from here."

So Stratton went back to his hotel to meet his Chicago detective. The latter had nothing to report. He told him the number of drug stores he had visited, but all without avail. No one had recognized the portrait.

"All right," said Stratton; "then you will just have to go ahead until you find somebody who does. It is, I believe, only a question of time and perseverance."

Next morning he arose late. He looked over the report of the trial in the morning paper, and then, turning to the leader page, read with rising indignation the following editorial:--

"THE BRENTON CASE.

"The decision of yesterday shows the glorious uncertainty that attends the finding of the average American jury. If such verdicts are to be rendered, we may as well blot out from the statute-book all punishment for all crimes in which the evidence is largely circumstantial. If ever a strong case was made out against a human being it was the case of the prosecution in the recent trial. If ever there was a case in which the defence was deplorably weak, although ably conducted, it was the case that was concluded yesterday. Should we, then, be prepared to say that circumstantial evidence will not be taken by an American jury as ground for the conviction of a murderer? The chances are that, if we draw this conclusion, we shall be entirely wrong. If a man stood in the dock, in the place of the handsome young woman who occupied it yesterday, he would to-day have been undoubtedly convicted of murder. The conclusion, then, to be arrived at seems to be that, unless there is the direct proof of murder against a pretty woman, it is absolutely impossible to get the average jury of men to convict her. It would seem that the sooner we get women on juries, especially where a woman is on trial, the better it will be for the cause of justice."

Then in other parts of the paper there were little items similar to this--

"If Mrs. Brenton did not poison her husband, then who did?"

That afternoon George Stratton paid a visit to Mrs. Brenton. He had hoped she had not seen the paper in question, but he hoped in vain. He found Mrs. Brenton far from elated with her acquittal.

"I would give everything I possess," she said, "to bring the culprit to justice."

After a talk on that momentous question, and when George Stratton held her hand and said good-bye, she asked him--

"When do you go to Chicago?"

"Madam," he said, "I leave for Chicago the moment I find out who poisoned William Brenton."

She answered sadly--

"You may remain a long time in Cincinnati."

"In some respects," said Stratton, "I like Cincinnati better than Chicago."

"You are the first Chicago man I ever heard say that," she replied.

"Ah, that was because they did not know Cincinnati as I do."

"I suppose you must have seen a great deal of the town, but I must confess that from now on I should be very glad if I never saw Cincinnati again. I would like to consult with you," she continued, "about the best way of solving this mystery. I have been thinking of engaging some of the best detectives I can get. I suppose New York would be the place."

"No; Chicago," answered the young man.

"Well, then, that is what I wanted to see you about. I would like to get the very best detectives that can be had. Don't you think that, if they were promised ample reward, and paid well during the time they were working on the case, we might discover the key to this mystery?"

"I do not think much of our detective system," answered Stratton, "although I suppose there is something in it, and sometimes they manage in spite of themselves to stumble on the solution of a crime. Still, I shall be very glad indeed to give you what advice I can on the subject. I may say I have constituted myself a special detective in this case, and that I hope to have the honour of solving the problem."

"You are very good, indeed," she answered, "and I must ask you to let me bear the expense."

"Oh, the paper will do that. I won't be out of pocket at all," said Stratton.

"Well, I hardly know how to put it; but, whether you are successful or not, I feel very grateful to you, and I hope you will not be offended at what I am going to say. Now, promise me that you won't!"

"I shall not be offended," he answered. "It is a little difficult to offend a Chicago newspaper man, you know."

"Now, you mustn't say anything against the newspaper men, for, in spite of the hard things that some of them have said about me, I like them."

"Individually or collectively?"

"I am afraid I must say individually. You said you wouldn't be offended, so after your search is over you must let me----. The labourer is worthy of his hire, or I should say, his reward--you know what I mean. I presume that a young man who earns his living on the daily press is not necessarily wealthy."

"Why, Mrs. Brenton, what strange ideas you have of the world! We newspaper men work at the business merely because we like it. It isn't at all for the money that's in it."

"Then you are not offended at what I have said?"

"Oh, not in the least. I may say, however, that I look for a higher reward than money if I am successful in this search."

"Yes, I am sure you do," answered the lady, innocently. "If you succeed in this, you will be very famous."

"Exactly; it's fame I'm after," said Stratton, shaking her hand once more, and taking his leave.

When he reached his hotel, he found the Chicago detective waiting for him.

"Well, old man," he said, "anything new?"

"Yes, sir. Something very new."

"What have you found out?"

"Everything."

"Very well, let me have it."

"I found out that this man bought, on December 10th, thirty grains of morphia. He had this morphia put up in five-grain capsules. He bought this at the drug store on the corner of Blank Street and Nemo Avenue."

"Good gracious!" answered Stratton. "Then to get morphia he must have had a physician's certificate. Did you find who the physician was that signed the certificate?"

"My dear sir," said the Chicago man, "this person is himself a physician, unless I am very much mistaken. I was told that this was the portrait of Stephen Roland. Am I right?"

"That is the name."

"Well, then, he is a doctor himself. Not doing a very large practice, it is true, but he is a physician. Did you not know that?"

"No," said Stratton; "how stupid I am! I never thought of asking the man's occupation."

"Very well, if that is what you wanted to know, here's the detailed report of my investigation."

When the man left, Stratton rubbed his hands.

"Now, Mr. Stephen Roland, I have you," he said.

CHAPTER XII.

After receiving this information Stratton sat alone in his room and thought deeply over his plans. He did not wish to make a false step, yet there was hardly enough in the evidence he had secured to warrant his giving Stephen Roland up to the police. Besides this, it would put the suspected man at once on his guard, and there was no question but that gentleman had taken every precaution to prevent discovery. After deliberating for a long while, he thought that perhaps the best thing he could do was to endeavour to take Roland by surprise. Meanwhile, before the meditating man stood Brenton and Speed, and between them there was a serious disagreement of opinion.

*   *   *   *   *

"I tell you what it is," said Speed, "there is no use in our interfering with Stratton. He is on the wrong track, but, nevertheless, all the influence we can use on him in his present frame of mind will merely do what it did before--it will muddle the man up. Now, I propose that we leave him severely alone. Let him find out his mistake. He will find it out in some way or other, and then he will be in a condition of mind to turn to the case of Jane Morton."

"But don't you see," argued Brenton, "that all the time spent on his present investigation is so much time lost? I will agree to leave him alone, as you say, but let us get somebody else on the Morton case."

"I don't want to do that," said Speed; "because George Stratton has taken a great deal of interest in this search. He has done a great deal now, and I think we should he grateful to him for it."

"Grateful!" growled Brenton; "he has done it from the most purely selfish motives that a man can act upon. He has done it entirely for his paper--for newspaper fame. He has done it for money."

"Now," said Speed, hotly, "you must not talk like that of Stratton to me. I won't say what I think of that kind of language coming from you, but you can see how seriously we interfered with his work before, and how it nearly resulted in his departure for Chicago. I propose now that we leave him alone."

"Leave him alone, then, for any sake," replied Brenton; "I am sure I build nothing on what he can do anyway."

"All right, then," returned Speed, recovering his good nature. "Now, although I am not willing to put any one else on the track of Miss Jane Morton, yet I will tell you what I am willing to do. If you like, we will go to her residence, and influence her to confess her crime. I believe that can be done."

"Very well; I want you to understand that I am perfectly reasonable about the matter. All I want is not to lose any more time."

"Time?" cried Speed; "why, we have got all the time there is. Mrs. Brenton is acquitted. There is no more danger."

"That is perfectly true, I admit; but still you can see the grief under which she labours, because her name is not yet cleared from the odium of the crime. You will excuse me, Speed, if I say that you seem to be working more in the interests of Stratton's journalistic success than in the interests of Mrs. Brenton's good name."

"Well, we won't talk about that," said Speed; "Stratton is amply able to take care of himself, as you will doubtless see. Now, what do you say to our trying whether or not we can influence Jane Morton to do what she ought to do, and confess her crime?"

"It is not a very promising task," replied Brenton; "it is hard to get a person to say words that may lead to the gallows."

"I'm not so sure about that," said Speed; "you know the trouble of mind she is in. I think it more than probable that, after the terror of the last few weeks, it will be a relief for her to give herself up."

"Very well; let us go."

The two men shortly afterwards found themselves in the scantily furnished room occupied by Jane Morton. That poor woman was rocking herself to and fro and moaning over her trouble. Then she suddenly stopped rocking, and looked around the room with vague apprehension in her eyes. She rose and examined the bolts of the door, and, seeing everything was secure, sat down again.

"I shall never have any peace in this world again," she cried to herself.

She rocked back and forth silently for a few moments.

"I wish," she said, "the police would find out all about it, and then this agony of mind would end."

Again she rocked back and forth, with her hands helplessly in her lap.

"Oh, I cannot do it, *I cannot do it*!" she sobbed, still rocking to and fro. Finally she started to her feet.

"I *will* do it," she cried; "I will confess to Mrs. Brenton herself. I will tell her everything. She has gone through trouble herself, and may have mercy on me."

"There, you see," said Speed to Brenton, "we have overcome the difficulty, after all."

"It certainly looks like it," replied Brenton. "Don't you think, however, that we had better stay with her until she *does* confess? May she not change her mind?"

"Don't let us overdo the thing," suggested Speed; "if she doesn't, come to time, we can easily have another interview with her. The woman's mind is made up. She is in torment, and will be until she confesses her crime. Let us go and leave her alone."

*   *   *   *   *

George Stratton was not slow to act when he had once made up his mind. He pinned to the breast of his vest a little shield, on which was the word "detective." This he had often found useful, in a way that is not at all sanctioned by the law, in ferreting out crime in Chicago. As soon as it was evening he paced up and down in front of Roland's house, and on the opposite side of the road. There was a light in the doctor's study, and he thought that perhaps the best way to proceed was to go boldly into the house and put his scheme into operation. However, as he meditated on this, the light was turned low, and in a few moments the door opened. The doctor came down the steps, and out on the pavement, walking briskly along the street.

The reporter followed him on the other side of the thoroughfare. Whether to do it in the dark or in the light, was the question that troubled Stratton. If he did it in the dark, he would miss the expression on the face of the surprised man. If he did it in the light, the doctor might recognize him as the Chicago reporter, and would know at once that he was no detective. Still, he felt that if there was anything in his scheme at all, it was surprise; and he remembered the quick gasp of the lawyer Brown when he told him he knew what his defence was. He must be able to note the expression of the man who was guilty of the terrible crime.

Having made up his mind to this, he stepped smartly after the doctor, and, when the latter came under a lamp-post, placed his hand suddenly on his shoulder, and exclaimed--

"Doctor Stephen Roland, I arrest you for the murder of William Brenton!"

CHAPTER XIII.

Stephen Roland turned quietly around and shook the hand from his shoulder. It was evident that he recognized Stratton instantly.

"Is this a Chicago joke?" asked the doctor.

"If it is, Mr. Roland, I think you will find it a very serious one."

"Aren't you afraid that *you* may find it a serious one?"

"I don't see why I should have any fears in the premises," answered the newspaper man.

"My dear sir, do you not realize that I could knock you down or shoot you dead for what you have done, and be perfectly justified in doing so?"

"If you either knock or shoot," replied the other, "you will have to do it very quickly, for, in the language of the wild and woolly West, I've got the drop on you. In my coat pocket is a cocked revolver with my forefinger on the trigger. If you make a hostile move I can let daylight through you so quickly that you won't know what has struck you."

"Electric light, I think you mean," answered the doctor, quietly. "Even a Chicago man might find it difficult to let daylight through a person at this time in the evening. Now, this sort of thing may be Chicago manners, but I assure you it will not go down here in Cincinnati. You have rendered yourself liable to the law if I cared to make a point of it, but I do not. Come back with me to my study. I would like to talk with you."

Stratton began to feel vaguely that he had made a fool of himself. His scheme had utterly failed. The doctor was a great deal cooler and more collected than he was. Nevertheless, he had a deep distrust of the gentleman, and he kept his revolver handy for fear the other would make a dash to escape him. They walked back without saying a word to each other until they came to the doctor's office. Into the house they entered, and the doctor bolted the door behind them. Stratton suspected that very likely he was walking into a trap, but he thought he would be equal to any emergency that might arise. The doctor walked into the study, and again locked the door of that. Pulling down the blinds, he turned up the gas to its full force and sat down by a table, motioning the newspaper man to a seat on the other side.

"Now," he said calmly to Stratton, "the reason I did not resent your unwarrantable insult is this: You are conscientiously trying to get at the root of this mystery. So am I. Your reason is that you wish to score a victory for your paper. My motive is entirely different, but our object is exactly the same. Now, by some strange combination of circumstances you have come to the conclusion that I committed the crime. Am I right?"

"You are perfectly correct, doctor," replied Stratton.

"Very well, then. Now, I assure you that I am entirely innocent. Of course, I appreciate the fact that this assurance will not in the slightest degree affect your opinion, but I am interested in knowing why you came to your conclusion, and perhaps by putting our heads together, even if I dislike you and you hate me, we may see some light on this matter that has hitherto been hidden. I presume you have no objection at all to co-operate with me?"

"None in the least," was the reply.

"Very well, then. Now, don't mind my feelings at all, but tell me exactly why you have suspected me of being a murderer."

"Well," answered Stratton, "in the first place we must look for a motive. It seems to me that you have a motive for the crime."

"And might I ask what that motive is, or was?"

"You will admit that you disliked Brenton?"

"I will admit that, yes."

"Very well. You will admit also that you were--well, how shall I put it?--let us say, interested in his wife before her marriage?"

"I will admit that; yes."

"You, perhaps, will admit that you are interested in her now?"

"I do not see any necessity for admitting that; but still, for the purpose of getting along with the case, I will admit it. Go on."

"Very good. Here is a motive for the crime, and a very strong one. First, we will presume that you are in love with the wife of the man who is murdered. Secondly, supposing that you are mercenary, quite a considerable amount of money will come to you in case you marry Brenton's widow. Next, some one at that table poisoned him. It was not Mrs. Brenton, who poured out the cup of coffee. The cup of coffee was placed before Brenton, and my opinion is that, until it was placed there, there was no poison in that cup. The doomed man was entirely unsuspicious, and therefore it was very easy for a person to slip enough poison in that cup unseen by anybody at that table, so that when he drank his coffee nothing could have saved him. He rose from the table feeling badly, and he went to his room and died. Now, who could have placed that poison in his cup of coffee? It must have been one of the two that sat at his right and left hand. A young lady sat at his right hand. She certainly did not commit the crime. You, Stephen Roland, sat at his left hand. Do you deny any of the facts I have recited?"

"That is a very ingenious chain of circumstantial evidence. Of course, you do not think it strong enough to convict a man of such a serious crime as murder?"

"No; I quite realize the weakness of the case up to this point. But there is more to follow. Fourteen days before that dinner you purchased at the drug store on the corner of Blank Street and Nemo Avenue thirty grains of morphia. You had the poison put up in capsules of five grains each. What do you say to that bit of evidence added to the circumstantial chain which you say is ingenious?"

The doctor knit his brows and leaned back in his chair.

"By the gods!" he said, "you are right. I did buy that morphia. I remember it now. I don't mind telling you that I had a number of experiments on hand, as every doctor has, and I had those capsules put up at the drug store, but this tragedy coming on made me forget all about the matter."

"Did you take the morphia with you, doctor?"

"No, I did not. And the box of capsules, I do not think, has been opened. But that is easily ascertained."

The doctor rose, went to his cabinet, and unlocked it. From a number of packages he selected a small one, and brought it to the desk, placing it before the reporter.

"There is the package. That contains, as you say, thirty grains of morphia in half a dozen five-grain capsules. You see that it is sealed just as it left the drug store.

Now, open it and look for yourself. Here are scales; if you want to see whether a single grain is missing or not, find out for yourself.

"Perhaps," said the newspaper man, "we had better leave this investigation for the proper authorities."

"Then you still believe that I am the murderer of William Brenton?"

"Yes, I still believe that."

"Very well; you may do as you please. I think, however, in justice to myself, you should stay right here, and see that this box is not tampered with until the proper authorities, as you say, come."

Then, placing his hand on the bell, he continued--"Whom shall I send for? An ordinary policeman, or some one from the central office? But, now that I think of it, here is a telephone. We can have any one brought here that you wish. I prefer that neither you nor I leave this room until that functionary has appeared. Name the authority you want brought here," said the doctor, going to the telephone, "and I will have him here if he is in town."

The newspaper man was nonplussed. The Doctor's actions did not seem like those of a guilty man. If he were guilty he certainly had more nerve than any person Stratton had ever met. So he hesitated. Then he said--

"Sit down a moment, doctor, and let us talk this thing over."

"Just as you say," remarked Roland, drawing up his chair again.

Stratton took the package, and looked it over carefully. It was certainly just in the condition in which it had left the drug store; but still, that could have been easily done by the doctor himself.

"Suppose we open this package?" he said to Roland.

"With all my heart," said the doctor, "go ahead;" and he shoved over to him a little penknife that was on the table.

The reporter took the package, ran the knife around the edge, and opened it. There lay six capsules, filled, as the doctor had said. Roland picked up one of them, and looked at it critically.

"I assure you," he said, "although I am quite aware you do not believe a word I say, that I have not seen those capsules before."

He drew towards him a piece of paper, opened the capsule, and, let the white powder fall on the paper. He looked critically at the powder, and a shade of astonishment came over his face. He picked up the penknife, took a particle on the tip of it, and touched it with his tongue.

"Don't fool with that thing!" said Stratton.

"Oh, my dear fellow," he said, "morphia is not a poison in small quantities."

The moment he had tasted it, however, he suddenly picked up the paper, put the five grains on his tongue, and swallowed them.

Instantly the reporter sprang to his feet. He saw at once the reason for all the assumed coolness. The doctor was merely gaining time in order to commit suicide.

"What have you done?" cried the reporter.

"Done, my dear fellow? nothing very much. This is not morphia; it is sulphate of quinine."

CHAPTER XIV.

In the morning Jane Morton prepared to meet Mrs. Brenton, and make her confession. She called at the Brenton residence, but found it closed, as it had been ever since the tragedy of Christmas morning. It took her some time to discover the whereabouts of Mrs. Brenton, who, since the murder, had resided with a friend except while under arrest.

For a moment Mrs. Brenton did not recognize the thin and pale woman who stood before her in a state of such extreme nervous agitation, that it seemed as if at any moment she might break down and cry.

"I don't suppose you'll remember me, ma'am," began the girl, "but I worked for you two weeks before--before----"

"Oh yes," said Mrs. Brenton, "I remember you now. Have you been ill? You look quite worn and pale, and very different from what you did the last time I saw you."

"Yes," said the girl, "I believe I have been ill.".

"You *believe*; aren't you sure?"

"I have been very ill in mind, and troubled, and that is the reason I look so badly,--Oh, Mrs. Brenton, I wanted to tell you of something that has been weighing on my mind ever since that awful day! I know you can never forgive me, but I must tell it to you, or I shall go crazy."

"Sit down, sit down," said the lady, kindly; "you know what trouble I have been in myself. I am sure that I am more able to sympathize now with one who is in trouble than ever I was before."

"Yes, ma'am; but you were innocent, and I am guilty. That makes all the difference in the world."

"Guilty!" cried Mrs. Brenton, a strange fear coming over her as she stared at the girl; "guilty of ***what***?"

"Oh, madam, let me tell you all about it. There is, of course, no excuse; but I'll begin at the beginning. You remember a while before Christmas that John came to see me one night, and we sat up very late in the kitchen, and your husband came down quietly, and when we heard him coming we put out the light and just as John was trying to get away, your husband shot twice at him, and hit him the second time?"

"Oh yes," said Mrs. Brenton, "I remember that very well. I had forgotten about it in my own trouble; but I know that my husband intended to do something for the young man. I hope he was not seriously hurt?"

"No, ma'am; he is able to be about again now as well as ever, and is not even lame, which we expected he would be. But at the time I thought he was going to be lame all the rest of his life, and perhaps that is the reason I did what I did. When everything was in confusion in the house, and it was certain that we would all have to leave, I did a very wicked thing. I went to your room, and I stole some of your rings, and some money that was there, as well as a lot of other things that were in the room. It seemed to me then, although, of course, I know now how wicked it was, that you owed John something for what he had gone through, and I thought that he was to be lame, and that you would never miss the things; but, oh! madam, I have not slept a night since I took them. I have been afraid of the police and afraid of being found out. I have pawned nothing, and they are all just as I took them, and I have brought them back here to you, with every penny of the money. I know you can never forgive me, but I am willing now to be given up to the police, and I feel better in my mind than I have done ever since I took the things."

"My poor child!" said Mrs. Brenton, sympathetically, "was that ***all***?"

"All?" cried the girl. "Yes, I have brought everything back."

"Oh, I don't mean that, but I am sorry you have been worried over anything so trivial. I can see how at such a time, and feeling that you had been wronged, a temptation to take the things came to you. But I hope you will not trouble any more about the matter. I will see that John is compensated for all the injury he received, as far as it is possible for money to compensate him. I hope you will keep the money. The other things, of course, I shall take back, and I am glad you came to tell me of it before telling any one else. I think, perhaps, it is better never to say anything to anybody about this. People might not understand just what temptation you were put to, and they would not know the circumstances of the case, because nobody knows, I think, that John was hurt. Now, my dear girl, do not cry. It is all right. Of course you never will touch anything again that does not belong to you, and the suffering you have gone through has more than made up for all the wrong you have done. I am sure that I forgive you quite freely for it, and I think it was very noble of you to come and tell me about it."

Mrs. Brenton took the package from the hands of the weeping girl, and opened it. She found everything there, as the girl had said. She took the money and offered it to Jane Morton. The girl shook her head.

"No," she cried, "I cannot touch it. I cannot, indeed. It has been enough misery to me already."

"Very well," said Mrs. Brenton. "I would like very much to see John. Will you bring him to me?"

The girl looked at her with startled eyes.

"You will not tell him?" she said.

"No indeed, I shall tell him nothing. But I want to do what I can for him as I said. I suppose you are engaged to be married?"

"Yes," answered the girl; "but if he knew of this he never, never would marry me."

"If he did not," said Mrs. Brenton, "he would not be worthy of you. But he shall know nothing about it. You will promise to come here and see me with him, will you not?"

"Yes, madam," said the girl.

"Then good-bye, until I see you again."

Mrs. Brenton sat for a long time thinking over this confession. It took her some time to recover her usual self-possession, because for a moment she had thought the girl was going to confess that she committed murder. In comparison with that awful crime, the theft seemed so trivial that Mrs. Brenton almost smiled when she thought of the girl's distress.

*   *   *   *   *

"Well," said John Speed to Mr. Brenton, "if that doesn't beat the Old Harry. Now I, for one, am very glad of it, if we come to the real truth of the matter."

"I am glad also," said Brenton, "that the girl is not guilty, although I must say things looked decidedly against her."

"I will tell you why I am glad," said Speed. "I am glad because it will take some of the superfluous conceit out of that French detective Lecocq. He was so awfully sure of himself. He couldn't possibly be mistaken. Now, think of the mistakes that man must have made while he was on earth, and had the power which was given into his hands in Paris. After all, Stratton is on the right track, and he will yet land your friend Roland in prison. Let us go and find Lecocq. This is too good to keep."

"My dear sir," said Brenton, "you seem to be more elated because of your friend Stratton than for any other reason. Don't you want the matter ferreted out at all?"

"Why, certainly I do; but I don't want it ferreted out by bringing an innocent person into trouble."

"And may not Stephen Roland be an innocent person?"

"Oh, I suppose so; but I do not think he is."

"Why do you not think so?"

"Well, if you want the real reason, simply because George Stratton thinks he isn't. I pin my faith to Stratton."

"I think you overrate your friend Stratton."

"Overrate him, sir? That is impossible. I love him so well that I hope he will solve this mystery himself, unaided and alone, and that in going back to Chicago he will be smashed to pieces in a railway accident, so that we can have him here to congratulate him."

CHAPTER XV.

I suppose," said Roland, "you thought for a moment I was trying to commit suicide. I think, Mr. Stratton, you will have a better opinion of me by-and-by. I shouldn't be at all surprised if you imagined I induced you to come in here to get you into a trap."

"You are perfectly correct," said Stratton; "and I may say, although that was my belief, I was not in the least afraid of you, for I had you covered all the time."

"Well," remarked Roland, carelessly, "I don't want to interfere with your business at all, but I wish you wouldn't cover me quite so much; that revolver of yours might go off."

"Do you mean to say," said Stratton, "that there is nothing but quinine in those capsules?"

"I'll tell you in a moment," as he opened them one by one. "No, there is nothing but quinine here. Thirty grains put up in five-grain capsules."

George Stratton's eyes began to open. Then he slowly rose, and looked with horrified face at the doctor.

"My God!" he cried; "who got the thirty grains of morphia?"

"What do you mean?" asked the doctor.

"Mean? Why, don't you see it? It is a chemist's mistake. Thirty grains of quinine have been sent you. Thirty grains of morphia have been sent to somebody else. Was it to William Brenton?"

"By Jove!" said the doctor, "there's something in that. Say, let us go to the drug store."

The two went out together, and walked to the drug store on the corner of Blank Street and Nemo Avenue.

"Do you know this writing?" said Doctor Roland to the druggist, pointing to the label on the box.

"Yes," answered the druggist; "that was written by one of my assistants."

"Can we see him for a few moments?"

"I don't know where he is to be found. He is a worthless fellow, and has gone to the devil this last few weeks with a rapidity that is something startling."

"When did he leave?"

"Well, he got drunk and stayed drunk during the holidays, and I had to discharge him. He was a very valuable man when he was sober; but he began to be so erratic in his habits that I was afraid he would make a ghastly mistake some time, so I discharged him before it was too late?"

"Are you sure you discharged him before it was too late."

The druggist looked at the doctor, whom he knew well, and said, "I never heard of any mistake, if he did make it."

"You keep a book, of course, of all the prescriptions sent out?"

"Certainly."

"May we look at that book?"

"I shall be very glad to show it to you. What month or week?"

"I want to see what time you sent this box of morphia to me."

"You don't know about what time it was, do you?

"Yes; it must have been about two weeks before Christmas."

The chemist looked over the pages of the book, and finally said, "Here it is."

"Will you let me look at that page?"

"Certainly."

The doctor ran his finger down the column, and came to an entry written in the same hand.

"Look here," he said to Stratton, "thirty grains of quinine sent to William Brenton, and next to it thirty grains of morphia sent to Stephen Roland. I see how it was. Those prescriptions were mixed up. My package went to poor Brenton."

The druggist turned pale.

"I hope," he said, "nothing public will come of this."

"My dear sir," said Roland, "something public will *have* to come of it. You will oblige me by ringing up the central police station, as this book must be given in charge of the authorities."

"Look here," put in Stratton, his newspaper instinct coming uppermost, "I want to get this thing exclusively for the *Argus*."

"Oh, I guess there will be no trouble about that. Nothing will be made public until to-morrow, and you can telegraph to-night if we find the box of capsules in Brenton's residence. We must take an officer with us for that purpose, but you can caution or bribe him to keep quiet until to-morrow."

When the three went to William Brenton's residence they began a search of the room in which Brenton had died, but nothing was found. In the closet of the room hung the clothes of Brenton, and going through them Stratton found in the vest pocket of one of the suits a small box containing what was described as five-grain capsules of sulphate of quinine. The doctor tore one of these capsules apart, so as to see what was in it. Without a moment's hesitation he said--

"There you are! That is the morphia. There were six capsules in this box, and one of them is missing. William Brenton poisoned himself! Feeling ill, he doubtless took what he thought was a dose of quinine. Many men indulge in what we call the quinine habit. It is getting to be a mild form of tippling. Brenton committed unconscious suicide!"

CHAPTER XVI.

A group of men; who were really alive, but invisible to the searchers, stood in the room where the discovery was made. Two of the number were evidently angry, one in one way and one in another. The rest of the group appeared to be very merry. One angry man was Brenton himself, who was sullenly enraged. The other was the Frenchman, Lecocq, who was as deeply angered as Brenton, but, instead of being sullen, was exceedingly voluble.

"I tell you," he cried, "it is not a mistake of mine. I went on correct principles from the first. I was misled by one who should have known better. You will remember, gentlemen," he continued, turning first to one and then the other, "that what I said was that we had certain facts to go on. One of those facts I got from Mr. Brenton. I said to him in your presence, 'Did you poison yourself?' He answered me, as I can prove by all of you, 'No, I did not.' I took that for a fact. I thought I was speaking to a reasonable man who knew what he was talking about."

"Haven't I told you time and again," answered Brenton, indignantly, "that it was a mistake? You asked me if I poisoned myself. I answered you that I did not. Your question related to suicide. I did **not** commit suicide. I was the victim of a druggist's mistake. If you had asked me if I had taken medicine before I went to bed, I should have told you frankly, 'Yes. I took one capsule of quinine.' It has been my habit for years, when I feel badly. I thought nothing of that."

"My dear sir," said Lecocq, "I warned you, and I warned these gentlemen, that the very things that seem trivial to a thoughtless person are the things that sometimes count. You should have told me *everything*. If you took anything at all, you should have said so. If you had said to me, 'Monsieur Lecocq, before I retired I took five grains of quinine,' I should have at once said; 'Find where that quinine is, and see if it *is* quinine, and see if there has not been a mistake.' I was entirely misled; I was stupidly misled."

"Well, if there was stupidity," returned Brenton, "it was your own."

"Come, come, gentlemen," laughed Speed, "all's well that ends well. Everybody has been mistaken, that's all about it. The best detective minds of Europe and America, of the world, and of the spirit-land, have been misled. You are *all* wrong. Admit it, and let it end."

"My dear sir," said Lecocq, "I shall not admit anything. I was not wrong; I was misled. It was this way----"

"Oh, now, for goodness' sake don't go over it all again. We understand the circumstances well enough."

"I tell you," cried Brenton, in an angry tone, "that----

"Come, come," said Speed, "we have had enough of this discussion. I tell you that you are all wrong, every one of you. Come with me, Brenton, and we will leave this amusing crowd."

"I shall do nothing of the kind," answered Brenton, shortly.

"Oh, very well then, do as you please. I am glad the thing is ended, and I am glad it is ended by my Chicago friend."

"Your Chicago friend!" sneered Brenton, slightingly; "It was discovered by Doctor Stephen Roland."

"My dear fellow," said Speed, "Stephen Roland had all his time to discover the thing, and didn't do it, and never would have done it, if George Stratton hadn't encountered him. Well, good-bye, gentlemen; I am sorry to say that I have had quite enough of this discussion. But one thing looms up above it all, and that is that Chicago is ahead of the world in everything--in detection as well as in fires."

"My dear sir," cried Lecocq, "it is not true. I will show you in a moment--"

"You won't show *me*," said Speed, and he straightway disappeared.

"Come, Ferris," said Brenton, "after all, you are the only friend I seem to have; come with me."

"Where are you going?" asked Ferris, as they left.

"I want to see how my wife takes the news."

"Don't," said Mr. Ferris--"don't do anything of the kind. Leave matters just where they are. Everything has turned out what you would call all right. You see that your interference, as far as it went, was perfectly futile and useless. I want now to draw your attention to other things."

"Very well, I will listen to you," said Brenton, "if you come with me and see how my wife takes the news. I want to enjoy for even a moment or two her relief and pleasure at finding that her good name is clear."

"Very well," assented Ferris, "I will go with you."

When they arrived they found the Chicago reporter ahead of them. He had evidently told Mrs. Brenton all the news, and her face flushed with eager pleasure as she listened to the recital.

"Now," said the Chicago man, "I am going to leave Cincinnati. Are you sorry I am going?"

"No," said Mrs. Brenton, looking him in the face, "I am not sorry."

Stratton flushed at this, and then said, taking his hat in his hand, "Very well, madam, I shall bid you good day."

"I am not sorry," said Mrs. Brenton, holding out her hand, "because I am going to leave Cincinnati myself, and I hope never to see the city again. So if you stayed here, you see, I should never meet you again, Mr. Stratton."

"Alice," cried Stratton, impulsively grasping her hand in both of his, "don't you think you would like Chicago as a place of residence?"

"George," she answered, "I do not know. I am going to Europe, and shall be there for a year or two."

Then he said eagerly--

"When you return, or if I go over there to see you after a year or two, may I ask you that question again?"

"Yes," was the whispered answer.

*   *   *   *   *

"Come," said Brenton to Ferris, "let us go."

The Codes Of Hammurabi And Moses
W. W. Davies

QTY

The discovery of the Hammurabi Code is one of the greatest achievements of archaeology, and is of paramount interest, not only to the student of the Bible, but also to all those interested in ancient history...

Religion   ISBN: *1-59462-338-4*   Pages:132

MSRP $12.95

The Theory of Moral Sentiments
Adam Smith

QTY

This work from 1749. contains original theories of conscience amd moral judgment and it is the foundation for systemof morals.

Philosophy ISBN: *1-59462-777-0*   Pages:536

MSRP $19.95

Jessica's First Prayer
Hesba Stretton

QTY

In a screened and secluded corner of one of the many railway-bridges which span the streets of London there could be seen a few years ago, from five o'clock every morning until half past eight, a tidily set-out coffee-stall, consisting of a trestle and board, upon which stood two large tin cans, with a small fire of charcoal burning under each so as to keep the coffee boiling during the early hours of the morning when the work-people were thronging into the city on their way to their daily toil...

Childrens   ISBN: *1-59462-373-2*

Pages:84

MSRP $9.95

My Life and Work
Henry Ford

QTY

Henry Ford revolutionized the world with his implementation of mass production for the Model T automobile. Gain valuable business insight into his life and work with his own auto-biography... "We have only started on our development of our country we have not as yet, with all our talk of wonderful progress, done more than scratch the surface. The progress has been wonderful enough but..."

Pages:300

Biographies/   ISBN: *1-59462-198-5*   *MSRP $21.95*

The Art of Cross-Examination
Francis Wellman

QTY

I presume it is the experience of every author, after his first book is published upon an important subject, to be almost overwhelmed with a wealth of ideas and illustrations which could readily have been included in his book, and which to his own mind, at least, seem to make a second edition inevitable. Such certainly was the case with me; and when the first edition had reached its sixth impression in five months, I rejoiced to learn that it seemed to my publishers that the book had met with a sufficiently favorable reception to justify a second and considerably enlarged edition. ...

Pages:412

Reference   ISBN: *1-59462-647-2*   *MSRP $19.95*

On the Duty of Civil Disobedience
Henry David Thoreau

QTY

Thoreau wrote his famous essay, On the Duty of Civil Disobedience, as a protest against an unjust but popular war and the immoral but popular institution of slave-owning. He did more than write—he declined to pay his taxes, and was hauled off to gaol in consequence. Who can say how much this refusal of his hastened the end of the war and of slavery ?

Law   ISBN: *1-59462-747-9*   **Pages:48**

MSRP $7.45

Dream Psychology Psychoanalysis for Beginners
Sigmund Freud

QTY

Sigmund Freud, born Sigismund Schlomo Freud (May 6, 1856 - September 23, 1939), was a Jewish-Austrian neurologist and psychiatrist who co-founded the psychoanalytic school of psychology. Freud is best known for his theories of the unconscious mind, especially involving the mechanism of repression; his redefinition of sexual desire as mobile and directed towards a wide variety of objects; and his therapeutic techniques, especially his understanding of transference in the therapeutic relationship and the presumed value of dreams as sources of insight into unconscious desires.

Pages:196

Psychology   ISBN: *1-59462-905-6*   *MSRP $15.45*

Dream Psychology
Psychoanalysis for Beginners

Sigmund Freud

The Miracle of Right Thought
Orison Swett Marden

QTY

Believe with all of your heart that you will do what you were made to do. When the mind has once formed the habit of holding cheerful, happy, prosperous pictures, it will not be easy to form the opposite habit. It does not matter how improbable or how far away this realization may see, or how dark the prospects may be, if we visualize them as best we can, as vividly as possible, hold tenaciously to them and vigorously struggle to attain them, they will gradually become actualized, realized in the life. But a desire, a longing without endeavor, a yearning abandoned or held indifferently will vanish without realization.

Pages:360

Self Help   ISBN: *1-59462-644-8*   *MSRP $25.45*

www.bookjungle.com *email: sales@bookjungle.com fax: 630-214-0564 mail: Book Jungle PO Box 2226 Champaign, IL 61825*

QTY

☐ **The Rosicrucian Cosmo-Conception Mystic Christianity** *by Max Heindel*   ISBN: *1-59462-188-8*   **$38.95**
The Rosicrucian Cosmo-conception is not dogmatic, neither does it appeal to any other authority than the reason of the student. It is: not controversial, but is: sent forth in the, hope that it may help to clear..   New Age/Religion Pages 646

☐ **Abandonment To Divine Providence** *by Jean-Pierre de Caussade*   ISBN: *1-59462-228-0*   **$25.95**
"The Rev. Jean Pierre de Caussade was one of the most remarkable spiritual writers of the Society of Jesus in France in the 18th Century. His death took place at Toulouse in 1751. His works have gone through many editions and have been republished...   Inspirational/Religion Pages 400

☐ **Mental Chemistry** *by Charles Haanel*   ISBN: *1-59462-192-6*   **$23.95**
Mental Chemistry allows the change of material conditions by combining and appropriately utilizing the power of the mind. Much like applied chemistry creates something new and unique out of careful combinations of chemicals the mastery of mental chemistry...   New Age Pages 354

☐ **The Letters of Robert Browning and Elizabeth Barret Barrett 1845-1846 vol II**   ISBN: *1-59462-193-4*   **$35.95**
by Robert Browning and Elizabeth Barrett   Biographies Pages 596

☐ **Gleanings In Genesis (volume I)** *by Arthur W. Pink*   ISBN: *1-59462-130-6*   **$27.45**
Appropriately has Genesis been termed "the seed plot of the Bible" for in it we have, in germ form, almost all of the great doctrines which are afterwards fully developed in the books of Scripture which follow...   Religion/Inspirational Pages 420

☐ **The Master Key** *by L. W. de Laurence*   ISBN: *1-59462-001-6*   **$30.95**
In no branch of human knowledge has there been a more lively increase of the spirit of research during the past few years than in the study of Psychology, Concentration and Mental Discipline. The requests for authentic lessons in Thought Control, Mental Discipline and...   New Age/Business Pages 422

☐ **The Lesser Key Of Solomon Goetia** *by L. W. de Laurence*   ISBN: *1-59462-092-X*   **$9.95**
This translation of the first book of the "Lemegton" which is now for the first time made accessible to students of Talismanic Magic was done, after careful collation and edition, from numerous Ancient Manuscripts in Hebrew, Latin, and French...   New Age/Occult Pages 92

☐ **Rubaiyat Of Omar Khayyam** *by Edward Fitzgerald*   ISBN:*1-59462-332-5*   **$13.95**
Edward Fitzgerald, whom the world has already learned, in spite of his own efforts to remain within the shadow of anonymity, to look upon as one of the rarest poets of the century, was born at Bredfield, in Suffolk, on the 31st of March, 1809. He was the third son of John Purcell...   Music Pages 172

☐ **Ancient Law** *by Henry Maine*   ISBN: *1-59462-128-4*   **$29.95**
The chief object of the following pages is to indicate some of the earliest ideas of mankind, as they are reflected in Ancient Law, and to point out the relation of those ideas to modern thought.   Religion/History Pages 452

☐ **Far-Away Stories** *by William J. Locke*   ISBN: *1-59462-129-2*   **$19.45**
"Good wine needs no bush, but a collection of mixed vintages does. And this book is just such a collection. Some of the stories I do not want to remain buried for ever in the museum files of dead magazine-numbers an author's not unpardonable vanity..."   Fiction Pages 272

☐ **Life of David Crockett** *by David Crockett*   ISBN: *1-59462-250-7*   **$27.45**
"Colonel David Crockett was one of the most remarkable men of the times in which he lived. Born in humble life, but gifted with a strong will, an indomitable courage, and unremitting perseverance...   Biographies/New Age Pages 424

☐ **Lip-Reading** *by Edward Nitchie*   ISBN: *1-59462-206-X*   **$25.95**
Edward B. Nitchie, founder of the New York School for the Hard of Hearing, now the Nitchie School of Lip-Reading, Inc, wrote "LIP-READING Principles and Practice". The development and perfecting of this meritorious work on lip-reading was an undertaking...   How-to Pages 400

☐ **A Handbook of Suggestive Therapeutics, Applied Hypnotism, Psychic Science**   ISBN: *1-59462-214-0*   **$24.95**
by Henry Munro   Health/New Age/Health/Self-help Pages 376

☐ **A Doll's House: and Two Other Plays** *by Henrik Ibsen*   ISBN: *1-59462-112-8*   **$19.95**
Henrik Ibsen created this classic when in revolutionary 1848 Rome. Introducing some striking concepts in playwriting for the realist genre, this play has been studied the world over.   Fiction/Classics/Plays 308

☐ **The Light of Asia** *by sir Edwin Arnold*   ISBN: *1-59462-204-3*   **$13.95**
In this poetic masterpiece, Edwin Arnold describes the life and teachings of Buddha. The man who was to become known as Buddha to the world was born Prince Gautama of India but he rejected the worldly riches and abandoned the reigns of power when...   Religion/History/Biographies Pages 170

☐ **The Complete Works of Guy de Maupassant** *by Guy de Maupassant*   ISBN: *1-59462-157-8*   **$16.95**
"For days and days, nights and nights, I had dreamed of that first kiss which was to consecrate our engagement, and I knew not on what spot I should put my lips..."   Fiction/Classics Pages 240

☐ **The Art of Cross-Examination** *by Francis L. Wellman*   ISBN: *1-59462-309-0*   **$26.95**
Written by a renowned trial lawyer, Wellman imparts his experience and uses case studies to explain how to use psychology to extract desired information through questioning.   How-to/Science/Reference Pages 408

☐ **Answered or Unanswered?** *by Louisa Vaughan*   ISBN: *1-59462-248-5*   **$10.95**
Miracles of Faith in China   Religion Pages 112

☐ **The Edinburgh Lectures on Mental Science (1909)** *by Thomas*   ISBN: *1-59462-008-3*   **$11.95**
This book contains the substance of a course of lectures recently given by the writer in the Queen Street Hall, Edinburgh. Its purpose is to indicate the Natural Principles governing the relation between Mental Action and Material Conditions...   New Age/Psychology Pages 148

☐ **Ayesha** *by H. Rider Haggard*   ISBN: *1-59462-301-5*   **$24.95**
Verily and indeed it is the unexpected that happens! Probably if there was one person upon the earth from whom the Editor of this, and of a certain previous history, did not expect to hear again...   Classics Pages 380

☐ **Ayala's Angel** *by Anthony Trollope*   ISBN: *1-59462-352-X*   **$29.95**
The two girls were both pretty, but Lucy who was twenty-one who supposed to be simple and comparatively unattractive, whereas Ayala was credited, as her Bombwhat romantic name might show, with poetic charm and a taste for romance. Ayala when her father died was nineteen...   Fiction Pages 484

☐ **The American Commonwealth** *by James Bryce*   ISBN: *1-59462-286-8*   **$34.45**
An interpretation of American democratic political theory. It examines political mechanics and society from the perspective of Scotsman James Bryce   Politics Pages 572

☐ **Stories of the Pilgrims** *by Margaret P. Pumphrey*   ISBN: *1-59462-116-0*   **$17.95**
This book explores pilgrims religious oppression in England as well as their escape to Holland and eventual crossing to America on the Mayflower, and their early days in New England...   History Pages 268

QTY

The Fasting Cure *by Sinclair Upton* ISBN: *1-59462-222-1* **$13.95**
In the Cosmopolitan Magazine for May, 1910, and in the Contemporary Review (London) for April, 1910, I published an article dealing with my experiences in fasting. I have written a great many magazine articles, but never one which attracted so much attention... New Age/Self Help/Health Pages 164

Hebrew Astrology *by Sepharial* ISBN: *1-59462-308-2* **$13.45**
In these days of advanced thinking it is a matter of common observation that we have left many of the old landmarks behind and that we are now pressing forward to greater heights and to a wider horizon than that which represented the mind-content of our progenitors... Astrology Pages 144

Thought Vibration or The Law of Attraction in the Thought World ISBN: *1-59462-127-6* **$12.95**
by William Walker Atkinson *Psychology/Religion Pages 144*

Optimism *by Helen Keller* ISBN: *1-59462-108-X* **$15.95**
Helen Keller was blind, deaf, and mute since 19 months old, yet famously learned how to overcome these handicaps, communicate with the world, and spread her lectures promoting optimism. An inspiring read for everyone... Biographies/Inspirational Pages 84

Sara Crewe *by Frances Burnett* ISBN: *1-59462-360-0* **$9.45**
In the first place, Miss Minchin lived in London. Her home was a large, dull, tall one, in a large, dull square, where all the houses were alike, and all the sparrows were alike, and where all the door-knockers made the same heavy sound... Childrens/Classic Pages 88

The Autobiography of Benjamin Franklin *by Benjamin Franklin* ISBN: *1-59462-135-7* **$24.95**
The Autobiography of Benjamin Franklin has probably been more extensively read than any other American historical work, and no other book of its kind has had such ups and downs of fortune. Franklin lived for many years in England, where he was agent... Biographies/History Pages 332

Name	
Email	
Telephone	
Address	
City, State ZIP	

☐ **Credit Card**   ☐ **Check / Money Order**

Credit Card Number	
Expiration Date	
Signature	

Please Mail to: Book Jungle
PO Box 2226
Champaign, IL 61825
or Fax to: 630-214-0564

ORDERING INFORMATION

web*: www.bookjungle.com*
email*: sales@bookjungle.com*
fax*: 630-214-0564*
mail*: Book Jungle PO Box 2226 Champaign, IL 61825*
or PayPal *to sales@bookjungle.com*

Please contact us for bulk discounts

DIRECT-ORDER TERMS

**20% Discount if You Order
Two or More Books**
Free Domestic Shipping!
Accepted: Master Card, Visa,
Discover, American Express

www.ingramcontent.com/pod-product-compliance
Lightning Source LLC
Chambersburg PA
CBHW082016170626
46817CB00009B/3119